I0592690

The Legend of the Gamesmen

The Birr Elixir

Book 1 of The Legend of the Gamesmen

Jo Sparkes

PORTLAND, OREGON

The Birr Elixir - Jo Sparkes – 3rd Ed.
ISBN 978-0-9853318-4-9

To Jackie, Meri, Sam, Kelly,

and most especially

to Ian.

.

And to Mike Terlizzi, for his wonderful maps.

Prologue

GREAT CONSTELLATION take you – FIND HIM!"

Beneath the yellow flowers, brambles sliced his hands. Climbing the rocky slope was tearing the flesh from his fingers. Tryst ignored the blood and pain, his eye on the shadow above him.

If it was a cave …

"We must bring proof – or there will be no gold."

Somewhere, behind him, Jason was trying to cover their tracks. Unless Jason – no. Jason wouldn't betray him.

Tryst ducked below the brush, wincing as thorns caught his hair, his clothes. His shoulder. Reaching the cave would only work if they never saw him enter.

If it was a cave …

Seven days earlier, he'd surveyed the east view from the council room.

Green hills, thick oak, blue sky. And wildflowers. All bunched up together, as if the mountain behind had pushed it all out of its way. It lacked the discipline of the palace gardens, but there was something Tryst liked about the sheer wildness of the view.

At one time, the King's council room had been open all around. The room was at the top of the palace, and should have commanded a superb view of Missea, the King's City. The seat and pride of the Skullan people. But over the thousand years since the first war, the arched openings had been sealed one by one, until only the east view remained. And the King's first minister urged that sealed as well. To protect King Bactor.

The door burst open and Tryst slipped behind the arch pillar, for all the world as if he were twelve instead of nineteen.

"Move the Devon garrison to Gold Harbor. It's the stepping stone to the city, and far too vulnerable." Even if the rasping voice hadn't revealed him, Tryst would have known Charis, the First Minister, by his words. Charis always wanted to prepare for battle – or to launch one.

"Too provocative, my friend," King Bactor's voice was strong, inspiring confidence. A true King's voice. "If we must do that – and I'm not convinced we must – let it be after the Comet Final."

And now Tryst felt like a foolish twelve-year-old playing hide and seek in his father's Council room.

"If they attack this year, they will fill the city during the Final. That's what I would do. We'd never count the troops until it was far too late."

"Do you think the Trumen are as clever as my First Minister?"

Tryst stepped out. His father saw him, but Charis had his back turned. The two stood on either side of the giant council table – a table surely meant, Tryst suddenly thought, for more than one adviser.

"I will defend my people." Bactor joined his son at the window, smiling warmly. "I will fight a war, if the stars steer it so, but I will not provoke one."

"The Chronicles –" Charis realized Tryst was in the room.

"Minister Charis." Tryst nodded.

"My Prince." Charis hid his annoyance well, but Tryst knew the First Minister didn't like to push the King in front of others. His father believed it was out of respect, but Tryst thought Charis preferred to keep his influence from being widely known.

None the less, it was widely known.

"We shall speak later, Majesty," Charis bowed again. "The Prince's epourney begins tomorrow, does it not? You will wish some time together."

Tryst waited until the First Minister was gone before grimacing.

"Minister Charis is a wise adviser. You would do well to appreciate him."

"Is war so close? Should I not remain?"

"According to Charis, war is always close. No, my son. The epourney is key to becoming a man, and a future King must first be a man."

"But I can help you. Everything I need to know I can learn right here in Missea -"

King Bactor burst out laughing. Tryst suddenly felt twelve again.

"You wish to rule the Skullan people without ever setting foot outside Missea? Without talking to them in their villages, standing beside them on their ships? You wish to decide the fates of Trumen without ever seeing who they are, how they live?

"Ignorance, my son. A blessing in a woman, a fault in a man. And a fatal flaw in a King."

All of Tryst's carefully marshaled arguments faded. Like it or not, he was going on the epourney.

The horses stood in the east courtyard. From here they would be relatively unseen as they departed. Though the mountains seemed impenetrable, there was a path that lead through them and beyond to the rest of the world. His father would say to the rest of the kingdom, but there were in truth whole continents unaware of the King's claim.

The path was long and difficult, which was why the castle was safe with the mountains guarding its eastern side. An army would march a long, dangerous trek, some of it single file, to use that access. They could carry nothing but what would fit on a horse, and find themselves very tired and thirsty before arriving. And they would be spotted hours before they reached safe cover.

Most visitors, of course, approached the other way, into the famous Gold Harbor. In the thousand years that Missea had stood, no one had ever successfully attacked the port. Only three had dared try.

Tryst had grown up with this lesson among the many. Not until today, however, did he come to appreciate it.

An epourney is undertaken with a best friend/companion, and a prince's epourney with no less than three. Baldar, Mauric, Jason, and five of the elite personal guard. He could have taken more – many more – but if he must do this journey, he preferred to travel light.

Jason had burst out laughing when he said that.

"What better way to see your kingdom than from behind a wall of armed men? How else can the citizens warm to you?"

Jason and Mauric were Tryst's best friends. He had eight prince-companions, but these two were good fellows, not afraid to make a joke or tell him he was wrong.

And today Mauric was late as usual. Jason calmed his spirited gray mount as a stable hand soothed Tryst's pretty white steed.

"Finally!" Tryst heard the oaken doors creak – but only Kellan emerged. Kellan was least of the prince-companions. A good political family, but in truth he shared not a common thought or opinion with the others. And he was a good ten years older.

"My Prince," Kellan bowed. "Mauric is taken ill this morning, and begs that I go in his stead. So that you may start your epourney at the appointed time."

"I don't think..."

"Kellan!" Baldar strode over to shake Kellan's hand. "Now we'll have some fun! My Prince, you must hear Kellan's newest trick. He's perfected a Minister Charis imitation."

They both waited expectantly, eyes sparkling with laughter. With confidence.

After the briefest hesitation, Tryst nodded.

It was only later he realized Kellan had mounted the dappled gelding. The horse he always rode. Mauric's black had not been brought to the courtyard.

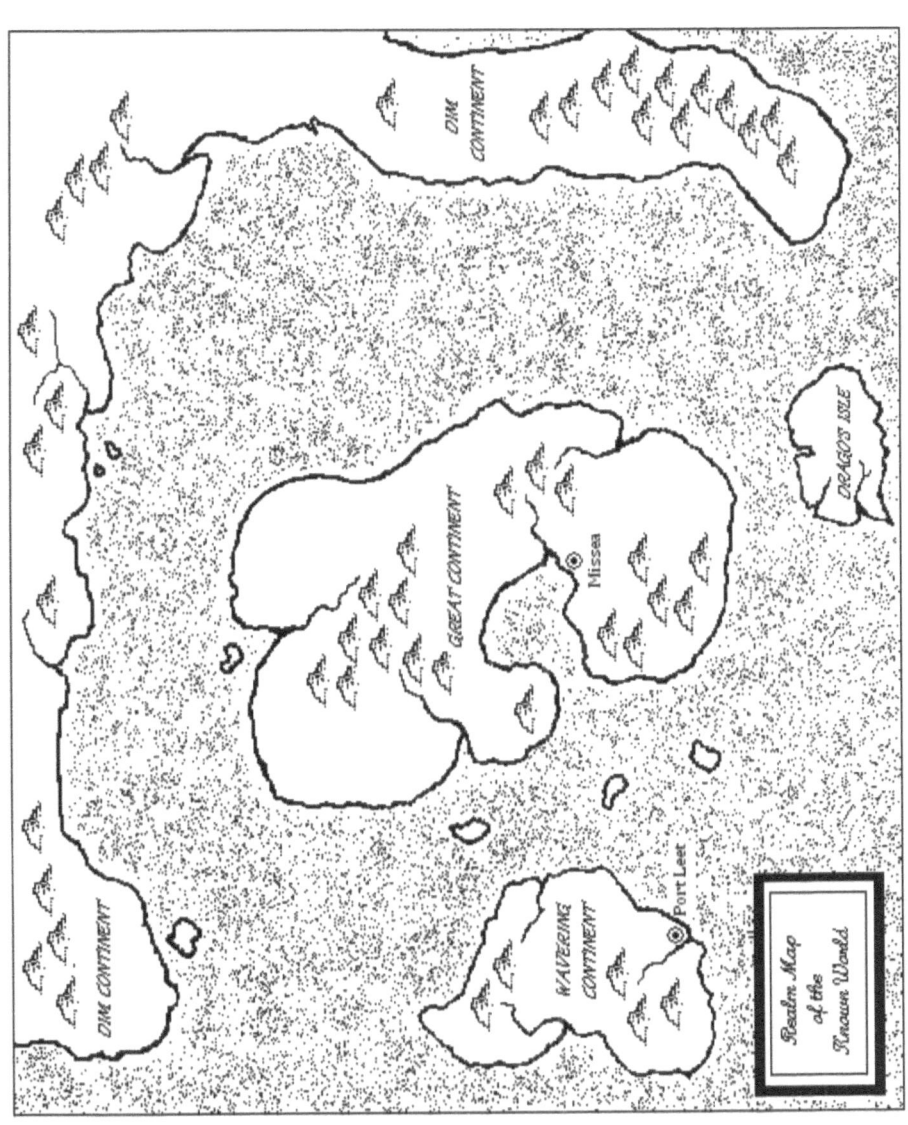

1.

I T WAS A VERY dirty shop.

Marra had long since given up trying to keep it clean. The dust of San Cris was the stuff of legend – and not in a good way. It had to be cleared out of your nostrils at the end of the day, or sleep was impossible. It clung to your hair, which was a reason so many women wore it short. Men wore their hair long, seemingly not to care that the sand actually lightened the shade. Most females preferred being clean.

Marra's dark red hair was long, and she spent a lot of time brushing the sand out. Some thought she was vain, and perhaps she was about the one thing that proclaimed she wasn't born in San Cris. But long hair was strength, the strength of warriors. And for Marra, it made her feel safer.

She wanted to feel safer.

At least it was a beautiful day, with that intense blue sky the desert had in the early morning, before the sun bleached the air white. And it was a comet day. If she hadn't already known there was a comet match this afternoon, the bustling street outside would have told her so.

She listened to the crowd noises now as she scraped the tiny leaves off the crys bark. And managed to scrape her thumb. Quickly she yanked away from the bowl, before the blood could ruin the herb.

And as she stood there sucking her thumb, in walked Drail, Leader of the 'Hand of Victory'. They must be playing today.

She snatched the injured finger from her mouth, covering it with her other hand.

Drail strode to the counter, getting bigger with each step. "Do you have an energy potion?" His eyes scanned the shelves behind her. And she blushed at the lack of wares.

There were herb jars, of course, but few mixtures. Marra was supposed to be an apprentice, learning the power of herbs, the alchemy of powders and potions to heal and en-hance. But Mistress Britta had died five weeks ago – just a year into her studies. And Snark, the Mistress's brother, had proved ignorant in the art.

"I'm sorry. Only a health tonic – to strengthen the diges-tion."

Drail's eyes roamed the shelves slowly, as if expecting to find some great elixir hidden amongst the cactus needles and crys bark. Marra wished there was something there to satisfy him, but she knew there was not.

"How long to make one?"

She stared back, unable to think of a reply.

"Please." He clasped both her hands with one of his, and she stared at the sheer size of his fist. There were rumors that Drail wasn't Trumen at all, but Skullan. Few really believed that, of course, for no Skullan would pretend to be other than Skullan. Besides, Drail had hair. Thick, brown hair tied in a long tail down his muscled back. Skullan had hairless bodies, and were much bigger than Trumen.

Drail was certainly big. And persuasive. "Please," he said, smiling at her. He leaned close enough she saw the brown flecks in his gold eyes. "Do you know what today is?"

"All of San Cris knows, sir. Comet day."

He shook his head. "All the comet days together would not equal this day. A Skullan team has entered the game."

Marra stared. "No Skullan would play a Trumen."

He shook his head. "Actually, there were at least six known games where Trumen faced Skullan. All six losses."

Marra had never heard such a thing. But she realized if anyone would know, it would be Drail. His whole family was legendary gamesmen.

"What's your name?" His eyes were sparkling – with excitement, she realized. No fear at all.

"Marra."

"Marra, seven is my lucky number."

Her own gaze dropped away from the sheer power of his. And alighted on the tome behind the counter.

It was Britta's Book, the mistress's handwritten collection of potions, balms, and notes. Snark wasn't even supposed to know about it, but she'd plucked it out to check proportions on a recipe and hadn't returned it to the hiding place. Besides, Snark rarely appeared until late afternoon.

Marra now lifted the heavy book onto the counter. It fell open as it always did at Britta's leaf-mark. On the BIRR ELIXIR.

"Yes!" Drail said, pointing at it.

"Birr?"

"Exactly! With that we will win!"

Marra had always assumed Birr was some sort of herb. Drail must know otherwise. Scanning the recipe, she saw only herbs she had. Except for something called Myrrcleft.

"Thank you, little Marra."

Her protest melted under his warm smile.

When she read it again, she realized that this Myrrcleft was probably the active ingredient. She could use basil. Basil had great mixing powers and could often be substituted, but if this was some sort of energy potion that may not be enough.

Then she remembered the Trevor seed. Mistress Britta had a two-fist sack filled with a tiny grain-like thing she called Trevor seed. Britta had said it 'boosted' things, made a potion more so of whatever it was to be.

Marra ran back to fetch one tiny seed. She crushed it with the mallet, releasing a sweet oily puff, and hastily dropped it into the elixir. Then she heated it as indicated, but not quite to boiling. Trevor seed lost potency in boiling, she remembered.

She poured the steaming liquid into a glass flask. Glass was expensive, but Britta had marked it must be so.

Hands grabbed her shoulders – she whirled to see Snark behind her. Something in his eyes made her stomach plummet.

"Special order," she nodded at the flask. "I have to take this to the field."

"Later," Snark stared at her blouse. He had been doing that lately, and it made her skin crawl.

"Drail said before the game – or no payment. It's for the Hand of Victory."

Snark's fingers slid over her shoulders. "I'll take it. You wait here."

"He said I must bring it myself." That was her second lie, and she winced inwardly. She'd never lied in her life until Snark became her boss.

But the lie worked.

"I bet he did," Snark grinned evilly. "Go, then. But don't be long. He's got game in an hour."

Marra raced out into the sunshine.

Travelers often referred to San Cris as outlying, which to Marra's mind meant small. It was one of the Sandy towns, out on the Flats of Beard. San Cris's population was less than two hundred Trumen total. And today it seemed twice as many were crowding the street, laughing and eating baked cactus treats. It was a comet day, and San Cris was the host.

For an instant Marra paused, weighing going back for her shoes against the possibility Snark would change his mind. To be barefoot marked one as poor indeed, but then that was pretty much what she was. So she defiantly tossed her long braid back over her shoulder, and hurried on.

She weaved her way through the crowd, then was suddenly snatched up off her feet as if she were a comet ball herself.

"Cute little Trumen," a booming voice said. Marra found herself face to face with a giant of a man, his head bald and the hollows surrounding his eyes painted dark green. His skin was pale – with patches of burning pink sunburn on his nose. And he had a spider tattooed on his cheek.

He had to be Skullan.

She'd never been so close to one before. By the Desert Crane, she'd only seen three of them in her whole life. Skullan were said to despise the desert almost as much as they despised Trumen.

"What a nice little prize," the Skullan leered. "You may warm my mouth now, and warm my lap later."

He pulled her closer. Marra instinctively braced both her feet against his chest. "You defy me, girl?" he asked softly. And she saw Bender, the old shopkeeper from down the street, lower his head and scurry past.

No one, she realized, was going to do anything to help her against a Skullan.

Her feet thrust out again before her brain could stop them. One foot skidded down his massive chest, scraping his nether region. He doubled over; Marra dropped to the dust.

Startled at his reaction, she hesitated but a second before seizing her good fortune. She scrambled to her feet and took off as his companion laughed.

She didn't slow down until a rock in her heel demanded attention.

The comet field was a huge circle of combed sand, with four perimeter posts set on the four compass points. Today those posts were decorated with streaming cloths of color tied to each. Marra passed the first post, with a dark green cloth the same shade as the Skullan eye paint, and quickly moved on to the red cloth, where Drail and three other Trumen warmed up. They were swinging powerful arms, kicking imaginary balls. When Drail saw Marra, he tapped a friend's shoulder before striding toward her.

She stared up at him. He had seemed so large in the shop, before she'd faced a Skullan. Drail had looked like a warrior in a tale come to life, but somehow seemed more human now that she'd witnessed the mass of a Skullan up close. She wanted to ask if he realized just how big they were. If he truly understood how difficult a game would be against such giants.

He must be the bravest man on the continent.

"Do you have it?" he asked with his easy smile. For all the world as if he'd forgive her if she didn't. Wordlessly she plucked the flask from her pocket, and only just realized how easily it might have broken in her scuffle. But it hadn't.

Drail removed the cork stopper, and glanced at her. "How much do I drink?" Most potions were intended to drink the whole amount at once. This one, she remembered, had been marked by the circle with the cross in the center.

"A quarter of it only."

"Perfect." Drail pulled a good drink from the flask, closing his eyes, savoring the feeling. After a moment he nodded. Marra hoped that meant it was actually working.

He then handed it to a teammate, a man even taller and with wild hair. When that one turned, she spied a lonely blonde curl dangling over his temple. Almost cute – if everything else hadn't been sinew and muscle.

"Manten. Drink a third, and pass it on," Drail told him. To Marra he tossed four coppers. "We offer you the post seat. You'll have a great view to watch your elixir at work."

She stared at the coins in her palm. "Too much, sir. It's only a copper."

"Four men. Four coppers." Drail gestured grandly toward the post, and she found herself moving before thinking. Behind him, his men donned comet leather, chest-jackets with a crudely drawn hand and a red "V". The sign of Drail's team – the 'Hand of Victory'.

Snark was waiting for her in the shop, and Marra trembled at the notion of disobeying him. But nearby spectators cleared the way before her, allowing her both the post spot and an unimpeded view. It was a true honor. A sort of respect she'd never experienced before.

There'd be hell to pay, of course. But that would come later.

And this was comet, after all.

Drail studied the field.

The center cone here was only high to a man's thigh, with the top cut off to make the hole wide enough to allow the ball to pass through the top with a finger's width to spare. This was the comet tail.

Comet was competition. Four teams of four men met in the arena, each with a chosen ball. The balls were covered with clinging soot-dirt, hiding the painted-on spots. To score, a ball must be thrown into the Tail.

A team could not score twice, but it could keep others from scoring, even up to sinking a second ball. That ball wouldn't count, and upon doing so the team had to retire from the field.

Beneath the soot-dirt the four comet balls were marked with 5, 3, 1, and no spots. The first team to sink a ball was awarded 3 points plus the point value of the ball; the second sunk ball was worth 2, then 1, and the last was 0 points. The longer you played, the more soot came off the ball, until the spots were revealed. But few in the Flats waited – for anything.

It was a wild game, with few rules. Players wore leather vests to protect themselves, but in truth the decorated material was more to mark the teams for the spectators than any real padding.

And for Drail, today was a landmark. It had been so long since Skullan had actually played against Trumen that it had become more legend than truth. He only knew of it because of his grandsire. Last night, when he'd seen the Skullan captain so obviously drunk, he'd baited him. Olver said he was wasting his breath; Manten had called him insane.

Today they faced not one, but two Skullan teams.

"TO THE FIELD!"

At the cry, Drail and his friends marched past the post, waving to the crowd. A comet game pulled people from a thousand spans, but even so it was hard to imagine how so many had appeared. San Cris was the smallest place he'd ever been that called itself a place.

The spectator roar was most satisfying.

"No one has ever beaten a Skullan," Olver said over the noise. Olver wore his black hair short, unlike most males. He claimed it practical for the sand of the Flats. But then, Olver was ten years older than any of his teammates, and far more jaded.

"There is a first time for all things," Kayle called back. Kayle was the youngest, and had yet to taste defeat. Kayle's hair was even blacker than Olver's, but worn long. When Drail had first seen him, Kayle's hair was braided. Braids were occasionally seen out on the Flats because few understood, much less observed, the conventions of a continent far away. Kayle had been accepted into the Hand of Victory once he changed the braid to a simple ponytail.

The four balls were at the comet tail, the center cone, watched over by the Judge. A Skullan Judge, Drail noted. The Skullan he'd suckered was making sure there would be no cheat.

Each team approached the comet tail. And the Skullan grew more enormous with each step.

"Stars!" Manten breathed. He was the tallest, yet the top of his head didn't reach as high as a Skullan shoulder.

At the inner circle, the line drawn in the sand around the comet tail, the teams halted. The Judge gestured, and Drail and the other Team Captains stepped over it. It was forbidden to cross the line without the Judge's approval. All scoring during the game had to be done from behind the line.

Drail glanced at the other Captains.

The Skullan radiated confidence. Contempt. They were sizing each other up – with barely a spare glance for the Trumen. The other Trumen Captain actually swallowed.

One Skullan, with a spider drawn on his cheek, picked up the ball in front of him. He'd made his choice. The second Skullan knocked the scared Trumen down to grab the ball beside him.

Drail chose the ball where the second Skullan had stood. He thrust it high over his head, spinning to face the crowd. A few murmurs rippled through the spectators as the fallen Trumen scurried over to the one remaining – barely grasping it before the Skullan whirled with balls held high. As the players trotted to the quadrant where their Captains held the ball, cheers erupted.

"They'll cheer for a Skullan win just as loud as ours," Olver yelled out over the noise.

Ball still held aloft, Drail strode to join his men. "Let's give them no opportunity," he said, as the Hand of Victory bowed to the crowd. And then turned as one to face the center.

Against the backdrop of the spectators, the sheer mass of the Skullan startled him. Tall they were, but more ominous was their breadth. The width of their shoulders seemed double that of any Trumen. Any bulging Skullan muscle looked the weight of three of his own.

Drail knew they were giants. He'd seen they were giants last night. But now his body felt the truth of the fact that his mind had continually glossed over.

"What do we do?" Kayle blurted out.

"Leave it to the Desert Crane," Manten grinned.

The Judge marched across the field to the raised platform at the edge. In the time it took him to climb the ladder, Drail could hear the breathing of his team. The whole arena had gone silent.

"United," he said.

"COMET!"

The Skullan charged the other Trumen team. Drail's team ran toward the Tail, Drail taking two steps and tossing the ball to Olver. There were no rules against one man running the ball in and scoring – but it was considered bad form.

Olver ran a short distance, then tossed it to Kayle. "They're ignoring us."

But they were not. Spider-Cheek and a teammate veered, sprinting towards them. "They don't want us to be first," Manten warned.

The Skullan were fast. In seconds they were there, thundering toward Kayle. He hurled the ball to Olver just before Spider-Cheek nailed him.

Drail heard the smack, saw the dust cloud. An instant later Olver was struck – and Spider-Cheek ran off with their ball, laughing with his companion.

"Great Crane!" Drail shook his head, to clear it as much as anything else, and then saw Kayle helping Olver – who was holding his shoulder.

Manten streaked out towards the Skullan. Drail sprinted after him. The Skullan took a shot at the Tail, but missed by a wide space. Briefly Drail wondered if accuracy was their flaw.

Manten dove into Spider-Cheek, driving him into the dust. Spider-Cheek roared in fury, and despite Manten's palm pin – a firm push on the small of the back that normally kept a man from rising - Spider-Cheek sprang up, shaking Manten off like a dog shook off sandfleas. Drail froze in awe.

WHAM - Drail dropped like a rock. The dust cleared from his vision, and he saw the ball that had nailed him. And the laughing Skullan who had thrown it.

The Skullan started towards the ball.

Drail rolled over onto his stomach, eyed the tail, and punched the ball with all his might. It flew towards the cone, over twenty paces away. It rolled up the side, up above the hole.

The whole arena held its breath as the ball seemed to hover mid-air.

And dropped into the cone.

The crowd erupted in pandemonium. It was a shot in a million.

On the far side of the cone, a Skullan from another team made his kick, trying for second score. The ball missed, hurling towards Drail's face.

Drail suddenly wondered if he had been the target of that kick.

He caught the ball, then scrambled upright. And raced towards the cone. Spider-Cheek sprinted to cut him off – but Drail drop kicked it on the fly. It would be considered a difficult shot, but a mere toss after that incredible punch score.

The ball went in.

"CEASE!" yelled the Judge. And the crowd went wild.

Spider-Cheek forced himself to stop. And from the look on his face, Drail was very glad he did. Another second and Drail would have had bones broken.

With the other players halted, Drail and his team retired from the field. "Well done!" the Captain of the other Trumen team called. Spider-Cheek glared.

A place was cleared for them, and the Hand of Victory gathered around their post. The game continued.

Marra stared up at them as the team surrounded her, but she doubted they were even aware of her presence. Drail and his men now watched the field, as if their sinking of two balls before a single Skullan comet was an everyday thing.

"COMET."

The game resumed. The crowd seemed to swell as those in the back tried to shove their way forward. Marra felt the heat on her face, the push of the people behind, and the sheer excitement in the air. She'd never forget this moment, never.

No Trumen ever beat a Skullan. No Trumen, ever, at anything. Had Drail and his friends actually done it?

She watched him, watching the game. His long ponytail hung down his back, almost blonde with its layer of San Cris dust. His muscles heaved as if he hadn't yet caught his breath. If she hadn't seen Skullan up close today, she'd wonder again if he wasn't one, hair or no hair.

She saw his nod before the crowd roared. The third and fourth ball had sunk - it was over. Comet games were never long – usually a quarter of an hour. But the intensity made you feel as if you'd run a marathon just watching a game.

Now the Judge marked a spot in the sand, beckoning. Drail and his men strode out to stand there as the crowd thundered its approval. The roaring continued as the Judge marked a second spot, and then a third, and a fourth.

The Skullan teams strode to the third and fourth spots. The other Trumen team quietly left the field. Failing to sink a ball was a disgrace.

The Judge marched to the Tail, plucked out the last ball to go in, and set that before the fourth team. Trudging back and forth, he plucked each ball free, and placed it in its mark.

The second ball on the second marker had no team. Marra realized this was the second comet Drail had sunk. Insuring no other team would be awarded points for that place, or that ball.

Everyone around her held their very breath as the Judge took a white cloth and cleared the soot from Drail's first place ball. Just as she made out the three circles painted on it, the roar broke out. The Judge drew a '6' in the dust at Drail's feet. The Hand of Victory had scored six points.

The second ball was wiped clean – it bore only one circle. Around her the crowd quieted. The 5 ball was still unaccounted for. If the third team had sunk the 5 ball, they would have six points as well.

The Judge placed the ball on the mark, and moved to the third team. The Skullan with the spider-cheek stood proud, as if he knew the ball was the five. A tie meant the two teams went back to fight it out.

The biggest injuries came from ties.

The Judge applied the no-longer-white cloth to the ball. There were no circles – it had no points. That gave a total of one point for the third ball. The last Skullan team had the five – but with no points for fourth place, it did them no good.

The very ground trembled with the shouts of the people. Drail merely smiled as if he'd won a simple game. He actually winked at her.

Stars, Trumen had actually beaten Skullan. And the tiny town of San Cris had the privilege of witnessing it.

Marra suddenly realized it would be very wise to get back to the shop. Comet games often led to wild times in the street, drinking and shouting and fights. An epic game could only mean epic celebrations.

She watched, horrified, as the Skullan with the spider-cheek strode over to Drail. He eyed him a long moment, before balling his fist and punching the Trumen's shoulder. Drail grinned and punched him back.

Marra was not the only Trumen to gasp in relief.

2.

WITH A FEW DEFT turns she avoided most of the crowd. It was only in stepping into the shop that Marra realized the worst might not be behind her at all.

Snark came through the back room door, and shut it behind him. In all her time there, she'd never seen the door closed. Stars, she hadn't even realized the door worked.

With a glance behind him, Snark shouted, "where have you been?"

"They would not let me leave until they saw that the potion had worked." She cringed at another lie, wondering what her mother would have said. Her fear of Snark was such that she found herself saying anything to avoid him.

"Did you bring back the vial?"

Of course – she should have retrieved the glass vial, which was expensive. But he'd paid her so much money, it didn't seem right. And – truthfully – she'd never thought of it.

She plucked the four coppers from her pocket, and set them on the counter. Snark's eyes widened.

"They won," she told him. "Drail won. They beat the Skullan."

"Now I know you're lying." Snark eyed the coins, but grabbed her shoulders. "You're no good with lies, girl. Trumen could not defeat Skullan, not in a thousand lifetimes." He studied her lips, much the way the Skullan on the street had done, and she wished beyond anything to kick Snark in the same manner.

"SNARK. This must be done quickly," a voice called from behind the closed door. Snark scowled, then shook her slightly.

"You go to my house, clean the floors. I'll be there after I – after I'm finish."

Twice before Snark had tried to get her to clean his place. Mistress Britta forbade it. In fact, she'd warned Marra never to set foot in Snark's house. Marra had always thought the Mistress had simply disliked her brother, but now she realized there was a whole different reason.

Her head was shaking 'no' even as she realized how he'd react.

He slapped her hard. "Do as I tell you, girl."

"Mistress Britta told me -"

This time he used his fist. The shop spun, and she saw the stars themselves when her cheek struck the floorboards.

Footsteps. She saw boots run by, heard the crack of a third punch that did not strike her. Another body hit the floor. And then gentle hands were lifting her up.

She hung limp, trembling. And realized the face peering into hers was Drail's.

"You all right? Girl?"

She nodded – mostly to answer him, so he wouldn't bother about her. And then she saw Snark out cold on the floor. "He'll kill me."

"We'll take you home," Drail told her. She tried to smile, and realized tears were flowing. She scraped them off with the heel of her hand.

"This is my home."

Drail frowned. She wanted to cringe away, but she did have some pride. "It's all right. Just don't be here when he wakes up. I'll tell him -"

"Get your things," Drail cut her off. "We wanted more of the Birr Elixir. Looks like we'll have plenty now."

The last sentence had been tossed over his shoulder. Marra looked – and saw one of his teammates behind him. The one with the short dark hair.

"Drail, you can't just take a girl. If she lives here, she's indentured or something. There would be hell to pay."

Marra rapidly weighed her options. "I'm not indentured. I'm apprenticed to Mistress Britta. It was an agreement be-tween my mother and her."

Drail raised an eyebrow. "Where is your mistress?"

"She died. Five weeks ago."

Snark wasn't moving – not even a groan. She started towards him, but Drail stopped her.

"Go get your things."

She could only stare at him. His friend did the same.

"Are you mad? We can't just take a girl!"

Drail smiled in such a reassuring way. "You'll be safe. I promise. Olver, she made the Birr Elixir. It wasn't on the shelf – she made it."

"Just what the hell is Birr Elixir? Never heard of it!"

Drail grinned. "A story my grandsire once told me. A powerful potion he used the day he played the Skullan."

Olver's eyes widened. Then he looked Marra over, and she realized he wasn't connecting her with any miracle drink. "Have you ever traveled with a girl? They want a mattress, they want to wash every day. They travel a third of the distance we do, insist upon rests."

Drail waved at her bare feet, and Marra's cheeks flamed. "I do not think she will hinder us much."

"At the least little snake they scream."

Marra wanted to protest that she did have shoes. Then her eyes settled on the unconscious man, and she knew beyond anything she wanted to wake up tomorrow miles away from Snark.

"I swear on the Desert Crane I won't hinder you." She sprang up the ladder to fetch her things.

On the loft platform that served as her room, she snatched up her mother's cloak – and then decided Snark would never miss the threadbare blanket. She tossed her spare blouse and single dress on top of it, and then gathered the four corners together for a makeshift bag. Grabbing the ends, Marra scrambled down the ladder.

Drail smiled, moving towards the door. Part of her wanted to simply follow him, but if she were to make potions she'd need supplies. Racing behind the counter, Marra hurriedly spread the blanket, and added a handful of glass vials and pottery jars, plus the two herb sashes, to her belongings.

And, lastly, Mistress Britta's Book. It was heavy and awkward, and she felt a qualm. But the Mistress had truly given it to her, just before the end. In fact she'd been made to promise Snark would not know about its existence.

She tied the corners of the blanket together. And then impulsively snatched two of the four coppers.

"Ready?"

Marra ran to the back room to fetch her shoes – and cried out.

A man lay on the back table, even more lifeless than Snark. He was young and large, maybe larger than Drail, and his hair was so short it appeared to be a mere shadow on his skull. If he'd been bigger she'd have thought him Skullan.

Drail and Olver stared from the doorway as Marra checked his breathing. Which was very shallow, but his color seemed good.

"He is alive, but deep in the twilight," she told Drail. And she wondered exactly what Snark was up to. This man was poorly dressed, but somehow seemed not so poor. His hair and nails were trimmed evenly, his complexion good. And there were no callouses on his hands. Marra had never seen a man without callouses on his hands.

Drail exchanged a long look with Olver, and then went down on one knee to hoist the sleeper up onto his shoulder.

"What are you doing?" Olver's voice rose with indignation.

"We can't abandon him here. When he wakes, he may even be grateful."

"You truly are mad."

Drail swept past Olver; Olver followed him out. Marra impulsively grabbed the small sack of Trevor seed, snagged her shoes, and sped after them.

It was dusk on the street, and the celebration was in full sway. "Drail!" a slender beauty called, offering a drink and more. He grinned and waved, but kept moving.

"We have an entire town celebrating our victory," Olver growled under his breath. "We should be helping them instead of a barefoot waif and an unconscious stranger."

Drail had to admit, the latter felt like a particularly heavy sack of scrub potatoes at harvest. "There's plenty of time to celebrate," he said aloud.

Olver sighed. "Have you even begun to wonder what's going on? What animal muck we've just stepped in?"

Drail glanced behind them – the girl was too anxious keeping up to mind their conversation. Still, he spoke low. "What would you have me do, Olver? Leave them both to the mercies of a sneaking coward who takes pleasure in beating the helpless?"

"Your helpless man looks very out of place to me."

Drail left the dirt road at the edge of the little town, striding through knee high brush. Dry brush, tinted pale brown in the waning sunlight, and with spikey edges that clung to their leggings.

"He wasn't robbed and left alone. Whatever they wanted from him, they weren't finished."

Drail paused. "They?"

"Unless you think that slimy old toad did it all on his own."

"We had no choice," Drail told him firmly. Or maybe he was telling himself.

They were camped outside of town, behind a large boulder that hid the fire from the path. The road was farther on, but if you traveled with less than five men in the Flats, you didn't sleep by the road.

Manten grinned and patted his lap when he saw the girl. Olver shook his head. Manten's grin faded as she stayed at the edge of the camp.

Kayle dragged firewood into the center. The desert of the Flats yielded few good logs – the most usable scraps were dried brush and small branches from crys trees. He checked upon seeing them. "Not the sort of guests I was hoping for." He did grin at the girl, the grin fading as she merely stared back.

Drail admitted to himself that he'd been impulsive. The stranger might be anyone, the situation anything, and he'd just waded in and took the man. He could almost see his father's frown.

But the girl at least was a find. He *knew* it - felt it in his bones. His grandsire had sworn his Brista made the difference between being good and being great. Few on the Flats had ever heard the term, much less understood its meaning. But on the Great Continent, a Brista was legendary and rare. She brought a strong distinction to a team.

At least according to his grandsire.

Drail nodded to a bedroll, and it was their Brista of two hours who hurried to smooth it out so he could drop the dead weight from his shoulder.

"Who is that?" Kayle stared down. "Is he Skullan?"

"A Skullan with hair?" Olver scoffed.

"They do have hair," Kayle retorted. "I got a good close look this afternoon. They must shave it off or something."

"Not tall enough for a Skullan," Drail eyed his guest judiciously.

"And how long are we to have the pleasure of his company?"

"Till he wakes."

Drail barely blinked when the serving maid set another pitcher on the table. She leaned close, allowing a lovely view down her gaping blouse, but he was too lost in thought to take note. She slammed the mugs down beside the pitcher and marched off.

All his life he had wanted to do what his grandsire had done. Not his father – his grandsire. To win the kind of prize money found only on the Great Continent. To travel the land of the Skullan, and earn their respect. To prove Trumen were not so inferior after all.

To win.

Raston, his grandsire, played his most famous game against a Skullan team. The Trumen had actually tied them, and the epic battle to end that tie had been set to song by the Skullan Prince himself. Such respect. Raston had been offered a house in Missea, a place to rival those of the Skullan elite. His grandsire had preferred to come home, he laughingly told to a very young Drail.

Drail had often pondered that choice. If he ever stood on the docks of Gold Harbor, walked the streets of Missea, and played in the Grand Arena, would he choose to leave? Raston had assured him that when his gaming days were over, it was the warmth of the desert sun and desert women that pulled a man home.

Perhaps. But it would be fantastic to have that same choice.

"So you did it. You actually defeated a Skullan team."

Drail looked up to see first the gamesman braid, iron gray though still thick with strength. Then he saw the cold black mustache and the warm blue eyes of Old Merle.

A slow grin broke out across Drail's face. "We did. We really did."

Merle sat, pouring half the pitcher into his own special mug. "Knew you were good. Didn't think you could do that. How did you do that?"

"You didn't see? You weren't there?"

"I was there. I saw you make a shot no one could make." Merle drank deeply, and then wiped a dribble from his moustache. "Your grandsire couldn't have made that – and he was the best. I'm damned sure you couldn't make it again."

Drail nodded. This was outside confirmation. "I think – I *think* – I have a Brista. She made a potion."

Merle drank again. Drail waited.

"A Brista. You think you found a Brista out here on the Flats."

Drail nodded.

Merle swished the beer in his mug, contemplating its froth. "Raston's Brista was a woman of Agben. Not a counter girl in an herb shop."

"There were rumors years back that Mistress Britta was a Woman of Agben. Marra is the only apprentice she ever accepted. That's got to mean something."

"It means you should leave her to apprentice."

"Britta died, Merle. I found this girl being turned into a drudge – or worse. She made me a Birr Elixir with her own hands."

"You asked for a Birr Elixir, and this girl just nods her head and gives you a drink?"

"I didn't ask. She opened a book – and there was the recipe."

Old Merle eyed him dubiously. "I'd wager she had no idea what it was."

"You admitted it was a shot Raston himself couldn't make."

"My grandson caught a wispwing yesterday. I'll wait 'til he does it a few times more before extolling his speed."

"But no Trumen ever defeated -"

Merle's cup slammed into the table. "Let's get one thing clear. When Raston – when we – played the Skullan, it was an honor bestowed on the greatest Trumen team to play the game. Only the two teams – no others were allowed to take the field that day. In the Grand Arena of Missea itself, there was no other competitor to distract – not Skullan or other-wise. It was a battle for the ages, young Drail.

"Yes, you won. The Hand of Victory won today – and it was quite an accomplishment. But don't imagine you some-how bettered Raston's feats."

Drail was still. Then, "my apologies, sir. It was foolish to puff off our win."

Old Merle met his eyes over the rim of his mug. And of-fered a slight toast. "It was a good win."

"Good enough to play Port Leet?"

"A chance," Old Merle drained his cup. "But consider this. Your victory was in a tiny village on the Flats, before a handful of spectators. And the only Skullan to see it won't be spreading the tale."

The moon was high beside the star-form of the Desert Crane when she heard the scrape.

Marra's first thought was Drail and his team were return-ing from the celebration. Then she heard a whisper and im-mediate hush, and her blood ran cold.

The instinct was to flee, but even with the urge whirling her body towards the open desert, her eyes fell on the still form. If Snark was looking for her, would he not also be look-ing for this man?

She squatted to push the sleeper, rolling him length-wise towards the brush. Stars, he was heavy. Her ears strained to catch any sound as her feet dug into the sand for traction. Time seemed frozen as the body slowly rolled, until he was half under the brambles. She scooped up handfuls of scattered leaves to toss on him.

Another scrape – this one much closer.

Too late to run now. Snatching a blanket, she dove under the large boulder to flatten herself between the dirt and the rock's overhang. A puff of sand surrounded her, and she clamped her palm over her mouth to keep from coughing.

A boot planted so near her face she could count the turns of the laces.

The man stood for a few seconds, then stepped away to the dying fire. Two more sets of feet – one in the sandal-shoes San Cris townsfolk wore – followed him.

"I told you," Snark's voice said. "They're at the pub."

"He was not at the pub." The accent was not like any she'd heard before. Deep, husky, and with a way of twirling the 'r's.

"Well, he can't walk now, can he?"

"The girl was also absent from the pub. He's with the healer."

"She can't heal, I keep telling ya. Her kind's good for one thing only."

"Her elixir served well enough against Skullan." Marra found herself staring at the boots – the fine workmanship, the gleaming leather. Few men wore boots in her life. And none of this quality. She stared at the hand-carved emblem on the inner ankle, sort of a rough outline of a fox.

When the man paced the other way, there was no emblem. The fox was only on the left boot.

Snark scoffed. "She's too stupid. The wench wouldn't have a clue about –"

"Your assurances that everyone else is stupid are starting to annoy me, Snark."

The boots turned and left.

The sandals hesitated. Marra didn't dare blink an eye.

"I'm telling ya," Snark began as the sandals hurried after the boots.

They were not so quiet leaving. She could hear them rounding the boulder, walking away. Even so, she stayed on her stomach between the rock and the sand.

3.

MARRA JERKED AWAKE to see more feet around the fire.

"Now where are they?" At Drail's voice, she hastily scrambled out. And confronted the four comet men with her dirty clothes and hair. By the Desert Crane, could she look any more pathetic?

Before she could speak, Manten rolled out the unconscious man. Drail touched her shoulder. "Marra? What happened?"

And tears sprung to her eyes. Her body shook, and her teeth chattered together.

"Oh, for -" Olver began, but Drail cut him off. "It's reaction."

The fire was made to blaze again, and a hot mug of tea shoved in her hand. Except when she took a drink, it wasn't tea at all. It was hot cider – three times as potent as beer. She tried to put it down, but Drail firmly pushed it back to her mouth.

Manten examined the mysterious sleeper. "He's still out. Stars, it makes no sense. He's exactly the same as when we left hours ago. Same breathing, same lack of movement. By now he ought to be awake or dead."

Marra found her tongue. "It's not natural, his sleep. There are potions to make one sleep like that." And she poured forth her story of Snark and the man with the fox boots.

"We don't need this," Olver told Drail.

Manten studied the unconscious man's face. "He's valuable to someone. How long before he wakes up?"

It took a few seconds before Marra realized he was asking her. "I don't know. There's one potion that puts a man out for a whole week – but others less time."

"Fine," Olver drained his own mug. "We leave him with the girl." He unrolled his pallet.

Wide-eyed, Marra looked at Drail. He smiled back with that gentle smile. Drail had a way of smiling from his heart straight to yours, she thought.

"Marra goes with us, my friends. She's our Brista."

Manten rose, unrolled another pallet. "Mistress," he bowed. She sat still, scared, until he produced a second pallet and climbed into it. Then, as she stood, she realized just how dirty she was. She brushed furiously at her clothes.

"And the Sleeper here? What's he – our lucky charm?" Olver seemed in no hurry to leave the fire.

"If these men want him so bad, we should see him safe," Drail tossed the rest of his mug into the fire, releasing a shower of sparks.

"And how do we do that, exactly? Carry him to San Tray?"

"We have prize money," Drail prepared his pallet. "We've got more things to carry. Time to buy a pony."

Marra awoke from a pleasant dream to see the sun had already broke the horizon. Anxiously she leapt up, only to realize where she was.

There was no Snark to scream if her chores weren't done. There was no floor to sweep, no orders to fill.

Manten and Kayle slept in their bedrolls. Drail and Olver were gone. And the unconscious one was exactly the same as she had left him.

Spying a kettle, Marra decided to fill it. The springs were not so far from their camp, and once she found them, she paused to clean herself as much as was possible without bathing. On her way back, she saw some Ragwort, and carefully gathered a handful of the best. Mistress Britta had taught her to take the purest leaves, but to make sure the plant itself was undamaged.

She realized she didn't have a sash, and hurried back to get one. It had been months since Marra had gone out into the desert without an herb sash – a long cloth of seven pockets for holding herbs. The cloth was then rolled up and tied, keeping its contents secure.

Back at the camp, the others still slept. She placed her herbs in the sash, and then checked the other pockets.

She had a few – very few – ingredients. There were enough to make the elixir once more, but she was going to need to gather if she was to serve Drail properly. As he deserved.

Setting the kettle to warm, Marra took the sashes out into the desert.

Mistress Britta's first lesson had been to gather. Plants and ingredients always grew where they could cure the ails of the area. That was a natural law. But the fancy potions, the things beyond cures, might need fancy ingredients. And some of these came from faraway places, with exotic sounding names.

When Drail and Olver returned, they led a bedraggled sand pony. Kayle protested vigorously, as he'd been envisioning four noble mounts, not one pack animal. Olver told him to save his breath. Fearing a fight, Marra was relieved when they quickly settled down to travel.

The men were eager to move on, to play the next comet game. Each sported a new cut in his comet sash. And they each now had ten cuts, she realized. Ten victories. They were officially 'gamesmen'. People would actually pay to see their play.

No wonder they were in a hurry.

It took more than twice as long to reach San Tray.

They spent a full week walking. Burdened with a heavy load, the pony plodded at a pregnant cow's pace, and all the yelling and smacking her rump couldn't change that. It took two days before Marra decided that Olver's complaints were directed at the pony, and not herself.

After she was sure, she relaxed. And realized there were plants all around, plants that she should be examining, valuing. She found clovesfoot and ragwort, and several for which she had no name. When a plant radiated a vibrant color, felt so alive, it had value. It took plants that thrived, not merely survived in the surrounding, to make good potions. The more vibrant, the more powerful.

The unconscious one did not wake nor change. Marra hadn't thought anything could keep a man sleeping like that. Not without re-administering. She searched Britta's book at night, trying to find a proper cure. But it was all guess work, and she was a novice.

Then she found mint, which was the basis for one such remedy, mixed in with thistle and the top leaf of summer weed. She brewed it all night, then tried it the next morning. But it was to be drunk, and he was not in a drinking sort of way.

She managed a little down his throat. But there was no effect.

An inhalant was a much more challenging recipe. She tried it, and this time he did seem to drift upwards, closer to consciousness. But in the end, the man still slept.

So she tried it again the next night, with a little mint and summer weed. And the next night she tried a Trevor seed. And on the next night – the last night of the journey – Marra tried all three.

The following morning he woke.

She'd fallen into the habit of being the first up. While the others slept she'd gather herbs and brew the tea. She had even tried cooking, but Olver preferred his own stews, and she found she had to agree.

She was just returning with more mint when she heard the groan. It wasn't the sound, but the direction, that startled her.

The unconscious one was actually sitting up. And cradling his head.

And eying her.

The water had boiled, so she quickly poured a cup of tea and scrambled over to drop to her knees.

He took the brew, staring at her. "How did you bring me here?" There was much anger in his voice. No confusion, just anger.

And he didn't repeat himself, as most men would. No shouting, no threatening gestures. He simply waited for her response.

It dawned on Marra that this man was from a very different world than her own.

"By sand pony, my lord."

His flash of anger was quickly controlled, but she feared it none the less. "Why?"

"We found you. Snark had you – and we could not leave you with him. He is not a good man."

She told him all she knew of Snark, and discovering him in Mistress Britta's shop. And when he asked, of San Cris, and Drail. He accepted everything but Drail's defeat of the Skullan. "I still don't know where I am."

"The Sandy towns. The Flats of Beard." He frowned at her as if none of those words meant anything at all. Marra impulsively added, "the Wavering Continent, on the –"

"Wavering Continent." He whispered the words, but she felt as if he'd shouted them. What deeds had Snark been doing?

The Man sipped his tea, staring off at worlds unseen. She waited, but he spoke no more. When the others stirred, she hurried to fetch their tea.

"He's awake," she whispered to Drail, handing him his mug. Drail merely grinned, rolling upright. "Well done," he told her. And strode off to talk to the man.

Hesitating only an instant, Marra followed.

The Man didn't say much. He asked Drail where they were, but seemed to have already accepted what Marra had told him. Drail offered to help him get home, but the Man didn't seem interested. He continued to stare off into space. The only further reaction from him was when Drail asked if he knew anyone in San Tray.

The Man actually laughed.

Around the fire the others stirred, and Drail turned to join them. He did throw one last question over his shoulder.

"What's your name, man?"

There was hesitation.

"Tryst," the stranger finally sighed. "I was Tryst."

Drail grinned. "You still are, friend."

By the time they reached San Tray, Marra was almost angry. The mystery of the Unconscious Man was something she'd worked to solve, and now felt due an answer. All she had was a name – Tryst. It had a foreign feel, a cloak of mystery all its own, but it certainly wasn't enough.

And Tryst offered no more. He asked questions, pondered answers. And then withdrew. She thought he was 'nobly sullen.' Olver had less kind words.

And she guessed when they reached the town, he'd disappear.

The Flats were flat indeed, so there were no dramatic changes in scenery. Only a handful of trees grew here, usually clumped together above some sort of underground water source. Shimmering mirages danced in the distance, appearing as the sun rose, fading away as it set. But the day they approached San Tray the mirages didn't fade. They turned into a town.

It took most of the day to reach the town. Tantalizing, to see San Tray slowly grow before them, resolving from shimmering light and vague buildings to streets and people. Drail and his team grew more excited with each step.

"Tray's Tavern," Manten grinned. "The Water and Whale. Best beer on the Flats."

And Marra saw it – a large, painted cloth hanging from a metal rod over a door. Painted with a frothing mug. Perhaps with so many buildings, the townspeople of San Tray found it necessary to mark which was which.

"Where are the real cities?" Tryst demanded. "Specifically a port on the sea?"

Until now, San Cris had been the only town Marra had ever seen. She knew it was small, but never really knew what that meant until standing on the edge of San Tray. What sort of place had Tryst lived that he could dismiss these bustling streets with such contempt?

Olver cut him a look, but Drail considered the question with his usual good grace. "Port Leet is weeks away. That's the only port on the Flats. Only place to even see the ocean."

Ocean. Marra's dad had shown her a bowl of water, and bade her lean her nose down to the edge and narrow her eyes until she saw only the sparkling surface. That was like the Ocean, he'd told her. She'd forgotten that.

San Tray's streets were lined with wooden platforms on either side, allowing you to walk above the sand. Here everyone wore shoes of cloth, and the cloth remained clean. The dresses were longer, too, hanging just at the ankle. At home the dresses were mid-calf, perhaps to help keep them out of the sand.

She looked down at her own skirt, frayed at the hem, and wondered how much a new one would cost. She had two copper, after all.

Tryst stared at the town with real horror. It was such a backwards settlement. Surely San Tray's entire citizenry was no larger than the palace staff.

When he'd first woke, he'd been furious. Someone had betrayed him; someone had betrayed the king. He was certain Minister Charis was behind it, and at least one of his own prince-companions had to have been involved. But more importantly, so had some of the Elite Guards.

And those same Guards were responsible for his father's life.

Worse, it was entirely possible his father knew nothing was amiss. Tryst's epourney was to have lasted a year or more – the King would be disappointed, but not surprised, if he received no letters for months.

"How long was I unconscious?" His hair had grown a good month's worth. He really needed his palace groomer.

She looked up at him. By the Great Missea Goose, she was so tiny. All Trumen were small to him, although with Drail and his men it was a welcome change. He was used to being the smallest in the room, and enjoyed being with men, even Trumen, who were his size. But with the girl – he feared a careless move would damage her.

Still, Drail and the others were obviously not concerned. Perhaps she wasn't quite as fragile as he feared.

"I do not know, sir." As always, she was quick to read his annoyance. "Truly. We found you unconscious, unnatural-like. It's been two weeks since we found you."

He grimaced, and scanned the streets for something to point his path. What to do next – how to get home.

"It is said in such sleeps, hair grows one tenth natural speed."

His gaze flew back to her. Surely she was prodding him, but she looked quite serious. Sympathy lit her eyes, and it made him furious. That a waif of a Trumen would feel sorry for him. That anyone would feel sorry for him. But the anger was drowned in a wave of doubt.

Ten months? Was it possible?

Stars, he'd been fighting for his life just days ago. It had to be just days ago. He remembered it so clearly, could even feel the beating. Subconsciously he held up his arms, remembering a guard swinging a tree branch, striking his forearm. Breaking a bone –

No bruises, he suddenly realized. There were no marks from that fight. And if he really was on the Wavering Continent, the sea voyage alone would be months. Stars, he wasn't even sure how long such a voyage was.

The girl was watching him so carefully. Nervously. And as he noticed the faces around them, the citizens walking the boards, entering the shops, Tryst realized there wasn't a Skullan among them. This girl, and Drail for that matter, were in no conspiracy against him. They were just Trumen happily going about their lives. If he spun around and strode away, they wouldn't try to stop him.

He really was on the Flats. On the Wavering Continent. As far from Missea as it was possible to be.

4.

KRATCHETT STRODE through the streets, eyes scanning the crowd. He didn't know any of the faces he sought – but he would recognize the group. It had been more than two weeks now, and they should be here.

It bothered him that Drail had taken the package. What was his motive? What did he hope to gain? Carting around an unconscious man was a nightmare in the desert, and by all accounts Drail's sole interest was comet.

Lump had mentioned 'compassion', and compassion was alien to Kratchett. Still, in his experience other men's compassion faded fast when that subconsciously expected reward did not appear.

He reached a corner – and spied Lump approaching from another street. Seeing him, Lump shook his head. Kratchett took a last scan around, and then entered the Whale and Water.

The Whale and Water – he'd actually laughed the first time he heard the name. Trumen loved double names for taverns, and never mind that this place was as far from the sea as it was possible to be. He doubted the barkeep had ever seen the ocean, much less a whale.

He spotted the San Cris fool at a corner table, and made his way through the empty chairs. The man was too busy drinking to even be aware of his approach.

"Enjoying yourself, Snark?" Snark spilled his beer.

"They ain't here, I tell ya. Are you sure this be the place they're heading?"

Kratchett sat, watching Snark wipe his fingers in the foamy suds on the table, then stick them in his mouth. "If you are certain it was Drail who took him, San Tray is his destination. There's a big game here tomorrow."

"Well, I ain't seen 'em."

"And what did the local Herb Woman say?"

"She's little better than a barmaid, far as I can see. 'Mint tea cures all' is her motto. She ain't seen nothing."

Kratchett sighed.

Lump slid silently into the last seat, setting two mugs on the table. "Barkeep ain't seen the skirt nor the comet leather. He'll tell me if he does." He hefted his ale, eying Kratchett over the rim. "And if our package is not sleeping anymore? He could be a week along the road to Port Leet, for all we know."

Kratchett grinned, taking a long drink. In a way, it would almost be worth it if the princeling was awake. That would certainly dim Rain's star. Still grinning, he plucked a handkerchief from his pocket, unwrapping it to reveal a tiny glass vial. "The sleep was – infallible."

Lump raised an eyebrow. "Seems to me we're spending that coin afore we've pocketed it."

"If he was awake, they would have been here by now."

"If they truly be coming here." Lump sipped daintily, a habit that fascinated Kratchett. "How long do we wait afore we say they ain't coming?"

Lump must have had a mustache at one time, Kratchett thought. That would explain why he took such care in his drinking. "If they're not at the game, we move on."

Looking down into his mug, Kratchett watched the others from his peripheral vision. "And if they are at the game, and you two hadn't found them before, there will be – compensation."

Lump's mug slowly lowered to the table. Snark, on the other hand, was still trying to fish the last few drops from a stingy glass.

Kratchett stood up. "Snark – you're the only one who knows what the girl looks like. They'll be needing supplies after traveling, and she's the logical one to fetch them. I suggest you find her."

Meeting Kratchett's eyes, Snark swallowed his protest.

Tryst entered the tavern to find it near empty. The barkeep smiled at him hopefully, the smile fading as Tryst strode up with a purposeful look.

"I need to get to Missea," Tryst told him.

The barkeep reached beneath the counter, pulling out a mug to set before Tryst. Empty as it was, the dust on it glittered.

"What will it be?" he asked. "Beside Gold Harbor."

Tryst shook his head. "How do I get there?"

The Trumen blinked, as if Tryst were asking the sum of one and one. And then he pointed east. "That way."

"I need men for escort. A capable guide. And horses."

The barkeep lowered his head, putting the mug back beneath his bar. When he looked up, Tryst was appalled to see he was laughing.

"And you have coin to pay for all of that, now do you?"

Instinctively Tryst glanced at his side. He had always had a man there, someone to pluck out payment or solve a problem. Or even to simply hold his steed. A companion who would have arranged their trip, knowing exactly how best to get them to Missea. Stars, he'd never been alone outside the palace. He wasn't sure he'd been alone below the chamber floors.

It dawned on him how fortunate it was that he'd turned down the offered drink. Tryst lacked so much as the copper to pay for it.

Just as Drail had said, the shop had a sign over the door. Five curling lines placed to illustrate a flower.

Marra entered, staring around at the second herb shop she'd ever seen. Although it looked grander on the outside, it was small on the inside, with less than ten large jars behind the counter.

The woman standing there frowned at her. Mistress Britta had taught Marra never to frown at anyone who walked through the shop door.

"How much for Myrrcleft?" she blurted out. Trying to let the woman know she had good business for her.

"Myrrcleft?"

"For energy," Marra said. A shadow moved behind the thin curtain to the back room, catching her eye because it went still when she spoke.

"Sorrel's better," the woman turned to reach down a jar. Marra doubted that, but held her tongue. The crumbled leaf the woman produced was long past its prime. "Four coppers."

Marra frowned at her. Drail's instructions had been to pay whatever the price, because things cost more in San Tray. But surely not for a useless weed.

"No thanks. Do you know where I can find Myrrcleft?"

The woman glared, but lapsed into sullen silence as a man stepped out from the curtain. "What be you needing energy for, girl?"

"A potion." He kept coming towards her, as if his conversation was merely to hold her in place. His hand reached out.

Falling back a step, Marra noticed his feet. They were shod not in the cloth shoes she'd seen here, nor in the desert sandals of San Cris, but in full boots. She couldn't see if these had a fox etched on the inner ankle.

She whirled and raced out the door.

"If you be knowing herbs, I might can use you – "

She sped down the wooden slats, darted around a corner, and then hid herself in a busy street.

Someone walked into their camp as they began the warm-up drill.

Drail beamed, brushing past a startled Marra. "Old Merle!"

"At what point did the 'Old' become part of my name?" Old Merle shook his head even as he clasped Drail's hand.

"Sir!" Manten stood, giving a tiny bow of respect. "Drail said you might join us."

"Thought it'd be a wasted journey," Merle nodded at the others. "So you're fighting after all?"

"After all? Did you think we couldn't get here in time?"

"I thought you were going to back out, like two other teams. No one wants to play the Sandflats team now. Not since they killed a man."

Olver and Kayle ceased their warm-ups. "What happened?" Kayle asked.

"Twas a head shot. Deliberate and vicious, but to my mind nothing I haven't seen before. It hit young Krittol square in the noggin. He dropped instantly, and never rose again."

"Krittol," Manten said.

Kayle sat, shaking his head. "No one's ever died before."

"Sure they have," Old Merle plopped down on a bedroll, eyeing the teapot. "Been a few years, is all. But it's bound to happen from time to time. Especially in the fever to get to Port Leet."

Marra fetched a mug, pouring him tea. The brew had grown strong, as she'd not removed the leaves, and there was no honey. Drail was ready with the apology. But Old Merle sipped and merely nodded appreciatively.

"I don't understand," Olver held out his mug, and Marra ran to fill it.

"Port Leet," Old Merle grinned. "The Summer Solstice game. It's in three weeks."

"That's where we're headed. It's a big honor to play in it," Drail said slowly. "But it's an honor to play at Port Leet at all. There's games every week."

"Story is, there's a Skullan team going to play Summer Solstice. Teams were shying off – no one thought it was possible to win. Then the rumor came: a Trumen team had beaten Skullan. If it can be done anywhere, they say, it can be done in Port Leet. Suddenly everyone wants their shot at it."

"As do we," Drail grinned, pounding Manten on the back. "To prove it was no fluke."

"No guarantees they'll let you play, son. Teams with a lot more wins than you demanding that honor. Hell, they won't believe you did it the first time."

A glass vial appeared before him. Marra held it aloft, seemingly nervous. Taking it, Drail smiled reassuringly, and stuffed the Birr Elixir in his leather.

"Are we still playing today?" Kayle asked. Manten and Drail exchanged a look, and burst out laughing; Olver slapped him on the shoulder.

"We play," Drail said, and stood up. And stretched. The others rose eagerly, Manten catching Kayle's eye.

"It's what we do."

Marra hesitated, and Drail knew she was wondering about Tryst. Their guest had left early, without saying anything, and hadn't returned.

"If he wants to find us, he will. The whole of San Tray will soon know where we are."

Marra stood in the front row, firmly clasping the rail so no one could move her. If teams were reluctant to play, spectators were that much more eager to watch. Her stomach was pressed against the wood bar as people squeezed closer to see.

San Tray's field was surrounded by wooden stands. She could see the whole field better than from her post seat in San Cris. Below her fluttered the red cloth of the Hand of Victory, tied to its post. The only familiar thing in a different comet field.

Suddenly a hand clamped over her mouth, and an arm snaked around her belly. "There you are," Snark said as he stepped before her, and she worried briefly who held her. "She's a runaway indentured," Snark announced to the crowd.

Frantically she bit the hand that silenced her. "I AM NOT!" she shrieked.

Snark froze in surprise, before stepping forward and smacking her hard. "Liar," he yelled for all to hear. "Bring her."

She suddenly realized Drail and the others would have no idea this was happening, no idea where she was until after the game. Perhaps long after.

And how much effort would they put in to find her? Especially if they lost? Marra began to struggle in earnest.

The spectators pulled back, making a hole around them, but no one interceded. No one would, she realized. She fought desperately, but the man behind held her firm.

A wild kick struck Snark's nose as he grabbed for her feet. Blood actually flowed. He wiped it, saw the red on his fingers. And grabbed her throat.

"You'll pay for that," he told her softly. She knew she would, ten times over. Even now the pulse pounded in her head as the grasp choked her. She couldn't breathe or see past her welling tears.

So she didn't know who shoved Snark aside, or punched the man holding her. Marra fell to her knees, which was a good thing as the man sailed over her head into the dirt arena.

Rubbing the moisture from her eyes, Marra barely had time to recognize the man in the dirt as the one from the herb shop before Snark landed on top of him.

"Get out of here, you lying jackals," Tryst snarled. "Marra is Brista to Drail's team. She is Brista!" he added loudly for the crowd's benefit.

Marra knelt at his feet, stunned. Stunned that she was safe, stunned that Tryst had not already left for his home. Stunned that he actually knew her name, let alone the term Drail called her.

And kneeling, she glimpsed another pair of leather boots in the crowd. Boots with an emblem of a fox on the inner ankle. They were a mere two arms-lengths away, frozen in place as the rest of the spectators moved.

Then Tryst plucked her up as if she were no more than a comet ball. She tried to peer around him – but he held her firmly, studying her eyes. "Are you hurt, girl?"

His piercing gaze riveted her own. She stared back, and after a moment, shook her head. Only then did he set her down.

And by then Fox-Boots was nowhere to be seen.

Kayle started to open the gate. With a wave of the hand, Old Merle stopped him.

"You wait," he said. For Kayle it just added to his disquiet.

Drail, however, continued stretching as if they were about to do a daily practice. "Who does the best leather fletching?" he called out. "I want a perfect O circling my ten marks."

Kayle shook his head. The O was etched in around the ten winning game marks, when the eleventh was won. The circles made it clear a team had won ten – or twenty, or even more – games.

How Drail could make such an outrageous assumption, when Krittol was dead –

Manten clapped him on the back. "You want this game?" His inflection implied it was a simple choice to make.

"CHALLENGERS COME FORTH!"

It sounded so formal, a challenge itself. The gate swung open.

It was said, Kayle suddenly remembered, the closer one went to Port Leet, the more people there were. San Tray held at least double, maybe triple, the crowd of San Cris.

Across the field he could see the three other teams, one of which was seasoned veterans. Drail recognized them, telling them over his shoulder that they had not played together as a team before. He speculated they'd joined together just to play this game.

Because no one wants to play the Sandflats, Kayle realized.

The second team, however, was both new and seemingly raw youth. While two of the four had strong physiques, they also kept glancing nervously at the Sandflats. Kayle knew he was guilty of the same thing, and forced himself to stop.

"APPROACH."

The Judge's voice somehow carried to the edges of the arena. Kayle hoped the man's eyes were as good.

The four team captains strode up to the circle. Three waited; the Sandflats Captain swept over the line, choosing to assume the Judge had granted permission.

The Judge's palm stopped him cold. "Wait," he told him. No hostility, but not allowing the man to dictate the course of the game, either. Drail smiled.

The Sandflats Captain saw the smile. His narrowing glare promised retribution.

"CHOOSE."

Now the four leaders stepped inside the circle. The Sandflats Captain snatched the ball in front of Drail, daring him to respond. The other two took the balls in front of them.

Drail let the silent arena crowd hold its breath. He slowly turned, as if making eye contact with every spectator. Then his toe hooked the ball in front of the Sandflats man, popping it up smoothly into his hands.

Chuckles rippled through the crowd. The Veteran Team Captain laughed aloud.

"What is he doing?" Kayle whispered.

"Bating him," Manten grinned.

"PLACES."

Kayle had never heard so many formal commands. At least there'd be no confusion on when to start – or stop. He watched the glower the Sandflats Captain riveted on Drail's back, as the captains strode towards their teams.

And suddenly Kayle got angry. These bastards killed Krittol, and instead of showing remorse were bent on scaring the rest of them. Expecting everyone else to back off.

He'd be damned if he'd back off from such cowards.

"COMET!"

Because he was watching them, Kayle saw the Sandflats Captain punch the ball with all his might, aiming for Drail's head. The collective gasp from the stands seemed to drain what little air remained in the heat.

Drail, expecting the move, caught the ball one-handed. Already sprinting for the comet tail, he now had two balls to sink. Realizing his intention, the crowd roared approval.

The youthful team seemed frozen in place; the Veteran Team was also on the move, but racing to block the Sandflats. They were out of position to stop Drail, and they knew it.

And the Sandflats – expecting a different reaction – had hesitated too long.

Drail reached the line, launching first one ball, then the other, at the comet tail.

Both flew in.

"CEASE." And the spectators leapt to their feet, shouting their appreciation.

Once Drail's Hand of Victory had retired from the arena, the game continued for a few blinks of the sun before the Veterans finally scored the third ball.

And buoyed by the play of their predecessors, the Youth team sprang to life, battling fiercely to stop the Sandflats from scoring. All young males could sink a comet ball, but few could defend the tail as these men suddenly did.

In the end, it was the Sandflats who left the field in disgrace.

The Youth came in second, sinking the three point ball in fourth place, causing a wild cheer. They were local, and about to become very popular. The Veterans were so enthusiastic that Kayle realized they must have sons on the team.

This time, however, Drail had sunk the five point ball first. The Hand of Victory had scored a perfect eight – within the opening blink of the sun. And in the celebration that ran long into the night, Old Merle made sure everyone knew this was the team that had truly beaten the Skullan.

"And if that doesn't land you a place on the Summer Solstice Game, I'm a copper-wench."

5.

THE SUN HAD SET, and the celebrations were still ramping up as Kratchett rubbed his horse down with straw. She was tall and black, but had a white smudge on her face, instead of the pure black of his Windstorm. Windstorm was in Missea, and his greatest possession.

She was a gift from a man he both loved and hated.

As he worked, he heard the stable door open. He glanced over his shoulder to see Lump and that useless shopkeeper Snark.

That bloody fool Snark.

"Not my fault!" Snark was arguing "You said he'd never..."

Kratchett spun and knocked Snark to the ground. His fat body made a satisfying thunk against the dirt – and his eyes looked like a cornered hare as he dared not meet Kratchett's gaze.

"You told me she had no skill."

Snark blinked, uncomprehending.

"One of the great women of Agben made that potion. An Agben sanctioned recipe. He should not be awake."

Snark crawled away, trying to get to his feet. "It must have worn off."

Kratchett kicked him. "An Agben sanctioned recipe? There was no wearing off." Tossing the straw aside, he untethered the mare and mounted. "We go," he told Lump.

Lump moved to the two ponies.

"Not Snark here."

"But the girl's mine! And my money –"

Lump swung into his saddle. Kratchett urged his horse forward to stand over Snark. Windstorm would have held perfectly still. With this unknown horse, it was necessary for Snark to hold perfectly still.

"You go home, Snark. And be thankful – be very thankful – that you live. Never tell this tale to anyone." At a touch of his heels the horse wheeled about, and then trotted out the door.

They were out of town before Lump drew up beside him. "And this sleeper? We just be walking now he ain't asleep?"

"It changes the terrain. I – need to rethink."

"And ye can't be thinking while following?"

Kratchett smiled his first smile since he'd beheld the prince-ling in full fighting form. "There is but one road home for him. Sooner or later, he must go that way."

Five days later they camped outside the next town.

It was early morning, and the other men slept. Tryst had no idea where the girl was. He emerged from the bushes nearby, and scanned the barren landscape. Looking for water, a place to get clean. But all he saw was dust.

To Tryst, sand was the white crystals on Gold Harbor beach. It warmed in the sun and crunched under foot. This sand of the Flats was a very poor substitute.

He spied the girl near a clump of crys trees. She was plucking leaves from a scrawny plant when he joined her.

"Is there a stream nearby?"

"I've already left water in the pot," she told him, obviously puzzled. Stars, these Trumen were so used to dirt, it never occurred to them someone might want to wash.

"I'd like to bathe." And when she frowned, "Wash this desert away."

And still she stared. Tryst opened his mouth to patiently try again, when her hand pointed to the trees. "There's a stream over there."

"Thank you."

"That's how you find water," she added. "The crys trees always cluster around it."

He smiled to think those were likely the most words he'd ever heard her speak at one time. "I don't know how you survive in this place. It's so barren of life."

Tryst could see she was genuinely puzzled. She rolled a stone, exposing a mossy substance on the underside. "There is much life," she told him, using a thin blade to scrape the substance into a pottery vial.

She worked so diligently, knowing so little. She'd never lived anywhere but the desert. How could she possibly understand how empty it was, if she'd never seen anything else?

A king must understand his people, he heard his father say. And for the first time in his life, Tryst thought his father might have been trying to do more than hold him back. Maybe the old man was as wise as the court whispered.

He would have spoken again, to draw her out, but she was looking so anxious. And he was feeling his dirt.

He went to the stream behind the trees, and finding it too small to submerge his legs, Tryst knelt to wash his face.

Marra heard the water splashing.

Mistress Britta had loved the fact that Marra's mother taught her to wash, which was not common in San Cris. Water was precious. But there were several springs near the town, so one could get clean with a little effort.

Traveling with Drail she had not always found the time, especially as he and his men were less fastidious. And she always felt guilty if she wasn't gathering herbs or helping the men.

She waited until Tryst had passed her, going back to camp. She waited until he couldn't possibly see her.

And then she scrubbed herself from hair to toenail.

Marra's new confidence was destroyed in the next town.

The population grew denser as one approached Port Leet, so towns were much more common. Naturally the next one had a comet game, and naturally Drail played.

And lost.

Suddenly all her deepest fears bubbled to the surface. She had no home to return to – her mother had left to find work after placing her with Mistress Britta. And when Drail finished with her, she'd have no skill to offer, for how could she claim to be good with herbs in a town where he'd turned off his Brista?

There was no talk of turning her off now, as he said the fault lay with a bad ball choice. The Hand of Victory had been the first to sink a ball, but the second team had sunk the five pointer. Sheer bad luck, Drail called it.

They lost the second game when another team outmaneuvered them.

This was in Turina, one of the bigger Flats towns. Being closer to Port Leet, the games were more important here. And they came in third, not second.

Marra stood by old Merle when it happened. The only words she'd ever spoken to him were 'more tea?', but here she was moved to cry out, "why?"

Old Merle looked at her a moment, and patted her hand. "There's natural gifts and talent, girl. There's developed skills. And there is also pure experience. Our lads have the talent, and are working on the skills. Experience – comes."

There were no recriminations thrown at her head, thank the Desert Crane. But there were bitter words around the fire that night.

"At this rate they won't let us play Port Leet." Olver had celebrated their first loss as hard as he celebrated their wins, but with this second one he remained in camp. As had the others.

"But we beat Skullan," Kayle said.

"And now two teams – no, *three* teams – can claim they beat us. Proving they're more capable of winning than we are." Olver kicked a stone, launching it into the campfire in a shower of sparks.

"It takes time to develop experience. You learn by playing the game," Old Merle said.

"Manten was slow on that block," Olver told the fire.

The others fell silent. Marra held her breath.

"And you stood by when Drail was first hemmed in," Manten told him.

"They held me as well."

"No they didn't."

"You move like a girl out there."

Tryst rose, stepping between Manten and Olver to rap a rag around the kettle handle. "Your problem," he told Olver, "is flat feet. You stand like a tree rooted to the ground, instead of on the balls of your feet, ready to spring in any direction. It takes you three times as long to move from flat feet."

Olver's jaw dropped.

"You too," Tryst glanced at Manten as he poured his tea. "Just to a lesser extent."

"I don't –"

"What about me?" Drail asked. There was no derision, no annoyance in his voice.

Tryst looked at him, and then nodded approval. "You move very well, with nice balance. Strong technique. But you don't watch the field."

Kayle rushed to his hero's defense. "He watches! He sees every move!"

Tryst kept his eyes on Drail, who merely waited. "Drail watches every move of the man in front of him. Locks eyes with him, even. You have to watch with your peripheral vision. See all men, not just the one in front of you."

"That's ridiculous!" Olver leapt to his feet, but Drail waved a hand. Drail was studying Old Merle's face.

Old Merle was staring at Tryst as if he'd discovered a Flatmouth viper in his bedroll. He spoke to Drail. "Your grandsire used to tell me that."

The others fell silent. Marra felt a slight thrill, as if she was responsible for Tryst's being there. Which was silly, of course.

"Who taught you all this?"

Tryst drained his mug, tossed the dregs at the fire. And grabbed his bedroll.

"A dead man."

To Marra's amazement, Drail insisted Tryst practice with them the next day. And Tryst did not want to. "I'm no gamesman," he said.

But gamesman or no, he showed Manten how to move on the balls of his feet. "You must be ready, all the time. Like a loaded spring. Active." Olver refused to participate, but he did watch the drill.

At the end of practice, Manten laughed. "I'm tired! This is hard work."

"Comet is a short game," Tryst told him. "And you do get used to it. Your body learns to use less energy."

He worked with Drail as well. "See who has the ball. You don't have to see faces, expressions. See the ball itself, where it moves, how it moves. See the guys behind, around."

"If you watch their faces, you sometimes see what they're thinking, "Olver scoffed. "What they're going to do."

"Against smart opponents, that can work against you. You can learn to fake a man by making him believe you're going to do something. Make him move one way while you go the other. It's what you don't see on the battlefield that will steal the victory."

"Battlefield," Kayle laughed. "You do take this seriously." Kayle was hesitant, like Olver, but watching carefully. At one point Tryst pointed at him and said, "You do this as well," and Kayle nodded ruefully.

It was a close-fought match.

Marra had given the elixir to Drail, anxiously watching his face. He smiled, as always. No hidden doubt, no accusations.

He even toasted her as he drank.

The teams in this game were better than the previous contests, and fought hard. Having watched the practices,

Marra could see when Olver was caught flat-footed, unable to stretch out for the ball, and unable to pursue his man. A big, screaming madman, who sunk the first comet.

And she could swear she saw Olver pale. He almost missed a ball Kayle tossed to him.

"PLAY!" Drail yelled. "We haven't lost yet!"

That seemed to spark them all, and even Olver rose up, no longer flat-footed. The madman grabbed a second ball, intent on sinking it as well, and this time Olver knocked him down.

It was Manten who scored. Two points, Marra told herself. But how many points on the ball?

The third ball was sunk by Drail. The madman had sort of quit, and was obviously startled at Drail's comet. Another team reacted angrily, which was foolish as that allowed the remaining team to sink the final ball. The team that sunk no comet had no place to stand when the judge determined the winner.

Marra held her breath as the judge pulled out the first ball.

"They played well, girl," Old Merle told her. "They have no need for shame. They're a worthy team." But he, too, leaned closer as the judge wiped the soot-dirt away.

The team of the madman, the first team to comet, had sunk the 1 point ball. With the placement points they had scored a 4.

"Interesting," Old Merle murmured.

Drail's ball was the three – for a total of five points. Marra cheered, then realized Old Merle was quiet.

Of course – because the five ball was still in the cone. If the last team to comet had sunk the five, they would be tied with Drail.

The third ball in – the ball Drail had sunk and thus no one got the points – was the five ball. That meant the last team to score had sunk the zero ball for no points.

Drail and the Hand of Victory had won the day.

"Persistence," Old Merle told her. "He never gave up."

Thus the feeling as the Hand of Victory trekked towards Port Leet was a good one. Drail's natural enthusiasm had reasserted itself, and while Old Merle reminded them there were many teams who wished to play, and Olver wished continually that they had never lost at all, they somehow expected to march into the arena for the big game.

When Old Merle announced they had arrived, Marra still saw only sand. He led them to three huge trees, beyond which she could see nothing. She just assumed it was another dip in the land.

It wasn't until she stood between the weeping branches that she saw. And froze in utter amazement.

The three trees stood guard along the top of a cliff. A single path sloped down a thousand paces to a mass of buildings, the largest town Marra had ever seen. And not mere dwellings with cloth roofs and narrow streets. Buildings stood atop buildings, with roofs as solid as walls. She couldn't begin to count them all. And all of it teeming with people.

Not a town at all, she told herself. A city.

And beyond the amazing city was water, as far as the eye could see. The same ocean of which her father had once told tales.

Marra now stood at the end of the land. Something she knew existed, because her father had said it was so. But she'd never actually expected to *see* it.

It scared her. The land really was finite after all. Somehow everything seemed suddenly limited.

Drail, Old Merle, and Tryst walked on as if it were nothing. As if they'd seen it many times before. Olver, Manten, and Kayle, however, had paused with her. Exchanging looks, she read the same doubts in their faces.

Then Olver stepped forward, following the others down. And they all continued on.

The path down was no path, really. It was wide enough ten men could walk abreast, and clearly beaten into the earth. In the desert it was rare to see footsteps in the sand, but on this road she thought she could see hundreds of them.

She really was leaving one reality, crossing into another.

And as they approached, the faint buzzing she heard grew. Turning into shouts, things moving, feet running. Such sounds as she had never imagined. So many people caused so much racket. There was no instinctive quieting, no dampening of the din. In the desert they did that. They were careful not to allow the noise of human existence sound too loud, in case predators of old were still seeking.

Here they dared them to come on. Marra wondered if that was very brave or very foolish.

6.

THE STREETS were laid stone. No dust rose up between the cut granite, and she realized there was a hard substance holding it all in place. How much work had gone into making these roads?

Old Merle led them down a large main avenue, passing a hundred people. Marra could only shake her head – she had no idea so many people existed. There was a line of men just waiting to enter a large building three stories high.

They joined the line.

"What is this?" Manten asked.

Drail smiled. "The line to register. To tell them we are here to play."

They stepped inside. When Marra turned, she saw two more groups had wandered up behind them.

Inside a heavyset man sat at a table, with paper – actual paper – before him. Behind him stood a massive wall, not quite thick enough to contain the sounds within it. Sounds Marra thought were faintly familiar.

The man raised a quill. "And you are?" Never before had there been so little interest in Drail.

"Hand of Victory," Old Merle said.

"He is Drail!" Kayle cried at the same time. "His grandsire was Raston!"

"I am Boric, Drail." The man dipped his quill in a cup, then scratched on the paper. Marra winced from the noise. "And every man here has a grandsire."

"We request the Solstice match," Old Merle told him.

"And your qualifications?"

"Drail's team is the only Trumen to have beaten Skullan."

The scratching stopped. "That's just a rumor," Boric said. He studied them from head to toe, and seemed to find nothing impressive. "A wild rumor."

"It happened. Out on the far Sandy towns."

"And who did you beat?"

"They gave no name. But the leader wore a spider on his cheek."

The sounds from behind the wall echoed on the high ceiling.

Boric lifted the pen and drew a hand beside his letters. And a 'V' on it.

Drail's eyes lit up as he saw it form on the paper.

"We shall consider," Boric said. "Pass."

And Old Merle led them through a large doorway into a huge chamber, big enough to dwarf the forty comet teams practicing in small clusters. The clatter echoed off the high walls as men slapped dirt, flesh, and occasionally the wooden wall.

"I don't want to practice here," Olver said. Old Merle shook his head.

"You must remain until the decision of where you play. And you would do well to drill instead of sit in the dirt."

They slowly took stances, stretched. Their eyes roamed the room, observing the others.

There was a Skullan team there, in the center area. And every other team was surreptitiously watching.

The center was dug deeper than the rest, shaped like the bowl of a giant comet field. Yet even sunken below the others, the Skullan were so massive compared to the Trumen around them.

They looked like men among boys. Watching their practice, Marra had no idea how anyone could ever defeat them. And judging by the faces of the other Trumen around them, she realized the thought was not hers alone.

Old Merle watched something else. Boric was now circling the room, talking to the other teams.

And those he spoke to were looking at Drail.

When one man grinned, Marra knew Drail would not get his wish.

Boric spoke to two more groups, and then approached the Hand of Victory.

"Have you played any of these teams?" he asked. Drail was still for a moment.

"Yes," he sighed. He pointed to four separate bands of men.

"And did you defeat them?"

"We defeated those two," Drail told him. Boric nodded, eyes noting the two Drail had not indicated. Then he turned to leave.

Old Merle pointed. "The Hand of Victory defeated them," he called out. An announcement, echoing around the room. Everyone turned to the entrance.

Spider-Cheek, the Skullan and his team, were entering the arena.

Boric froze; Drail grinned. And seeing Drail's grin, Boric scurried over to the new arrivals.

Spider-Cheek frowned, and looked up across the arena. And locked eyes with Drail. No one could hear his reply, but Boric stared after him as the Skullan pushed on to the center area.

Marra determined to find Myrrcleft somewhere in this great city. Because Drail would play the Skullan again, and she dare not let him down this time.

She'd roamed the desert many times, gathering herbs. But roaming the streets was different.

For one thing, the sheer size of Port Leet was daunting. Most towns were a few streets away from open desert. But here she could walk and walk, in any direction, and still be surrounded by buildings. And wood ones, too. Wood wasn't common in the desert. Things were constructed of sand-brick, a mixture of sand and water and Cactus sap, all cooked in a large iron oven. And roofs were often sky cloth – a special cloth treated with rain oil, which repelled water yet allowed enough sun through to light up the room.

Here even the roofs were wood. And wood could burn, unlike sand-brick, yet the city used a stunning amount of flame as its people stayed up late into the night. Other towns used candles, of course, but not on this scale. Only the San Cris pub used them to keep going after dark – and even there, a brazier provided most of the light. To burn so many candles seemed indecent.

Marra actually felt nervous when she rounded yet another corner, only to confront more stone walks and three-story buildings. Where was that herb shop?

And then, at the end of the next street, she saw a hanging board over a far door. The board showed a painted glass beaker.

She hurried up the street and inside.

The shop was smaller than her own in San Cris, which made her feel better for some reason. Until she saw the rows of shelves lining the walls. All the way up to the ceiling, and each laden with glass or pottery jars. And these jars bore labels such as 'energy', 'love', 'tooth', and 'sailor's complaint'.

Mistress Britta kept only three prepared potions in her shop. The rest were made to order, because they lost potency after weeks on the shelf. Marra's mind boggled at the idea of selling so much that you could keep all this ready made in advance.

There were a dozen people in the shop.

"And some of that hair syrup," an older lady told the boy behind the counter. The boy poured a small amount from a bottle into a tiny pottery vial, and set it beside a beaker and a cloth sack tied in a knot.

"Twelve copper, mistress," the boy said. Marra doubted Mistress Britta took in twelve copper in an entire week. This lady merely counted out coin, as if such large amounts meant nothing to her.

When her turn came, Marra still hadn't seen any labels for what she wanted. Or indeed, for any ingredient.

"Do you have Myrrcleft?"

The boy blinked. He turned to stare at the jars, but Marra had already scanned them twice. "Maybe in the back? I didn't see it up there."

Another blink, and the boy finally disappeared behind the curtain doorway. And returned five minutes later empty-handed. "Gran will be with you in a moment. Mistress Matton, how is your son?"

Marra had time to read all the shop's labels again before the curtain twitched. Then a gnarled hand clutched it, and the boy turned to answer a whispered summons. And nodded. And called to Marra.

"Go behind the curtain," he told her.

She hesitated a few moments, and then went.

The old woman behind the curtain was gaunt, almost skeletal – yet full of life. She looked Marra up and down for a full thirty seconds before speaking.

Somehow Marra didn't dare speak first.

"What did you ask for?"

"Myrrcleft, Mistress."

Her eyes seemed to bore through to Marra's soul. "And why would you be wanting that?"

"Do you have it, Mistress?"

"Answer my question, missy."

Marra had sought Myrrcleft in other places, and no one knew what she was talking about. Now she suddenly wondered exactly what it was she'd been seeking.

"I have a tonic to make -"

From the old woman's reaction, Marra might have said she used it to fly through the skies.

"Did Britta send you?"

Marra was silent – but her face must have said much. "How is Britta?" the old woman whispered.

"She died, ma'am. Almost three months back."

The old woman didn't blink, and Marra thought she hadn't heard. Then the tiniest sigh escaped the dried lips.

"Ohhh, Britta."

A pitcher of water sat on a crude table. Marra glanced around for a cup, and found one upside down on a shelf.

She filled it and brought it back.

For a few seconds, the old woman didn't move. And just as Marra thought of fetching the boy, the gnarled hand grasped the cup. She sipped gently, then handed it back.

"You're a kind one," she said. "The apprentice?"

Marra nodded.

"Britta never told you of Myrrcleft, girl."

"It's in her recipe. Her book—"

"Faugh!" the old woman screeched. "You can read?"

Marra only stared back. In San Cris, she realized, only her mother and Mistress Britta could read. And her mother had warned her once not to tell people. But the farther they went on the Flats, the bigger and more sophisticated the towns had seemed until Port Leet itself, a vastly superior city.

She'd thought everyone was so much better – so much smarter – than she was. Marra had just assumed they could all read.

"Who are you, girl?"

"Marra, Mistress."

"Who were your parents?"

"My mother was a dressmaker."

"On the Flats?"

Marra nodded – but the old woman was staring at the floor, thinking. "She couldn't have made any money there. Where did she come from? Who were her parents?"

When the old woman's eyes bored into her, Marra could only shake her head. The old woman sighed then, muttering, "I'd give a lot to see that recipe."

Marra opened her mouth to offer to fetch the book.

"Now shut up and listen to me, girl. Never mention that herb again. It don't exist on the Wavering Continent, and where it does exist, few know the name. And those that do –"

Marra swallowed.

"Before you get any ideas of basil, don't. Myrrcleft is a very rare bulbous root, much stronger. And just knowing that could land you in a pile of trouble."

"I've been using basil. And Trevor seed."

The old woman cackled. "I see why Britta chose you. Careful girl – Britta's Trevor seed is treated to boost its power. I don't know how she did it, but if you go back to regular Trevor seed the effect will be cut in half. And Trevor's only on the Great Continent - don't grow here. You'll recognize the plant when you see it – leaf has that odd stripe just like the seed.

"Gather that yourself – never ask for it."

Gran leaned closer, as if some unseen person might overhear. "And mind, Missy. If you ever get your hands on Myrrcleft, stick to the original recipe. Don't mix it with Trevor seed."

Marra left through the back door with a packet of Illsmith. It was an ivy Marra had thought of as wanderlust, and Gran swore it was made for healing muscles from the Game. "A pinch in a palm-full of oil when body parts ache. Rub well, until the skin feels hot. Half that in a glass of water when he aches all over. He drinks it quick, and then he swallows nothing more for an hour."

"Thank you, Mistress."

"Faugh, girl. Just you mind what I said."

She'd feared the old woman when she first beheld her, but now Marra hated to leave. Gran, as she told Marra to call her, was the first one to know things since Mistress Britta.

"Mistress Gran," Marra began.

"Just Gran, girl. And don't say anything. I'd be tempted, and that's not where your path lies."

Hesitating a moment, Marra finally nodded and left.

Out the back door, she had almost reached the turn of the alley when hands snatched her up. A foul smelling scarf clamped over her mouth, and with barely a whimper she was stolen away.

7.

THE ROOM WAS SMALL – two beds stacked above two beds, four pegs, a cold brazier, and a window. Yet it meant more than the finest room in the finest inn. It was a coveted berth above the Port Leet Arena.

Drail found himself just standing in the doorway, grinning like an idiot. How many times had his grandsire told him of sleeping here? Of how that privilege had to be earned, and how very few did so.

"A little straw in the corner will do for me," Old Merle was telling them. "Tryst can sleep by the door."

"You'll sleep there," Drail pointed to a lower bed. "One of us will take the straw."

"And our Brista?" Olver asked. He took a step towards the second lower bunk and then stopped, waiting for Drail's choice.

With a grin, Drail tossed his gear on the upper bunk above Merle's. Sleep above wisdom, he told himself. "Our Brista stays in the Brista quarters."

"All to herself," Merle added. "Bristas are rare on the Flats." He threw his satchel on the bed, glanced around, and chuckled. "Enjoy it, men. Only twelve Arena rooms, and those rarely filled. 'Tis an honor to sleep above the arena."

Manten marched up to the other upper bunk, tossed his bag, then threw back his head and yelled, "KYYYYRRRRRRAAAAA!"

It echoed off the walls, the ceiling. Off their beings. Kyra, the ancient battle cry. Said to be used before battles against the Skullan of old; used by Drail's grandsire before he stepped on the field of the biggest comet game of his life. No one had dared use it since.

Drail touched Manten's arm. "That belongs to Raston."

Manten grinned, unrepentant.

Barely an hour earlier, they had stood with all the competitors, practicing and waiting. Boric, the heavyset man with the quill and the page, had finally finished his rounds. He marked his paper, tallying tick marks, while every gamesman waited and tried to pretend not to care.

At last Boric moved to a raised judge's platform. "The Solstice Games are in seventeen days," he said. And Drail thrilled to hear the words, spoken in a normal tone yet easily reaching the farthest man from the speaker. Raston had told of the arena's startling build, where a judge could whisper and all would hear. This was the indoor arena, but the outdoor, which was built above them, supposedly had the same sound-carrying build.

"There will be seven games that day. Sixteen teams will play in the first four. The top two teams in each of those games will play in the next two. And the top two of those will play in the Solstice Champion Game."

"That's the first time they let sixteen into the Solstice," Old Merle murmured.

"Six of those sixteen have already proved themselves worthy. Ten more must still do so, and will be granted the chance the day after tomorrow."

The four Skullan teams were in the six. A Trumen team that was almost legendary, that had defeated Drail handily on the journey to Port Leet, was also in the six.

And the last team to make it, to be called by Boric, was the Hand of Victory.

Now Drail could stand here all night, staring at this prized room, hardly believing he would sleep in the same bunk as many a famous gamesman. As Raston and his men.

But Old Merle had been here before, and was thinking of his stomach. "There's at least a dozen taverns I well remember. One in particular with great ale and a nice hot kettle meal."

"My purse may not bear these city prices," Kayle told him.

Old Merle clapped his back. "With Boric confirming your victory over Skullan, every man in Port Leet will be eager to hear the tale. I doubt you'll spend coin on so much as an ale your whole time here."

Kratchett heard the barn door slide.

Lump carried her in, somehow managing to shut the door without freeing her. But then she'd long stopped struggling, if she had struggled at all. Her type often submitted to whatever woe life presented.

The girl's eyes were lowered, staring at his boots, when she suddenly jerked free of Lump. Lump merely let her go, ready to catch her if she ran. But her eyes remained fastened on his boots.

Kratchett supposed she'd only seen sandals in her desert life.

"Your name is Marra, is it not?"

Slowly her eyes shifted to his face. She made no acknowledgment.

"Marra," he smiled. "No need to fear me. You're here because you have a chance to serve Missea – a well-paid service. The man that travels with you now is a declared enemy of the King."

Still no reaction – and her unblinking stare began to bother him. Lump eyed her as if he'd discovered a Flatmouth viper in his bedroll.

Kratchett stepped close to tower over her. Her eyes remained on his, her chin lifting. But now he could see the tremor in her hands – and was satisfied.

"His true name is Vrull. He hasn't told you that, I'd wager. He's escaped from the Dim Continent."

"There is no Dim Continent. That's a child's tale."

Kratchett moved to an empty stall, relaxing against the rail. "Ask Tryst if the Dim Continent is real." When she made no answer, he continued. "Vrull – Tryst – is a petty princeling there. He left to seek our weak points, to forge the best maps, best plans for invasion. His own father has recalled him, having no wish to battle the Skullan realm.

"But he refuses his own sovereign, seeking instead to do damage from within. We would execute him, but his father has made a royal plea of the King. Send his son home, and he shall never leave the Dim Continent again. Fail – and King Bactor's own son will be forfeit. This he has sworn on the Zaria Scrolls."

Marra's gaze was unfocused, as if she saw through him. He found himself almost nervous, which was ridiculous. Kratchett knew he had the upper hand.

At last she spoke. "What would you have me do?"

He reached into his coat, plucking out a crystal vial. "All of this into his food or drink. It will not harm him, only put him to sleep. We'll do the rest."

She stepped towards him, then hesitated.

He produced a second crystal vial. "The carrot for the sand pony, little Brista. This vial contains Myrrcleft."

Finally a reaction. Her eyes widened, and her hand reached for it instinctively. "Enough to last a long time. I doubt you'd find another vial on the whole of the Wavering Continent."

She did take it, weighing it carefully, touching the wax sealed stopper. He would swear she was checking it to see if it was real, except he knew she'd never seen Myrrcleft in her life. He offered the sleeping vial, and still she resisted.

"The sand pony also needs a stick, Brista. We must capture Vrull, without harming him. You can make that very easy for everyone; without your help we must resort to rougher means. If Drail were to get in the way –"

Her eyes met his, and he actually thought he saw contempt before they lowered. He would have slapped her hard enough to drop her, if he didn't know he'd already won. She would never let harm come to her meal ticket, especially now that she had that rarest of ingredients to insure her life as a Brista.

Marra took the second vial from him, not meeting his eyes.

Lump tossed a colorful scarf at her feet. "When the deed is done, wear that outside the arena. We will find you."

She snatched the scarf and hurried to the door, waiting for Lump to open the heavy portal. When he had done so, she rushed out without a backwards glance.

Tryst looked out over the wharfs.

Twenty ships bobbed in the water at that very moment, tethered together by thick rope and thin gangplanks. Most were big with two tall masts, and one had three, but there were smaller boats as well.

Surely someone would take him home.

He strode through the activity. Crates and barrels suspended by ropes or hoisted on shoulders and carted away. Men sweating in the afternoon sun, working and shouting to peers and bosses. Dock workers, he realized. Missea had the famous Gold Harbor, where he had also strolled the planks. With everything so different here, he hadn't expected the docks to be exactly the same.

In Missea he'd walked with Jason, who had explained about the great sails carrying the heavy ships. "Remember this," Jason had told him. "The sail is the lightest, the least of the sailing vessel. It's fragile, as the big ship and strong oak masts are not. Yet without the sail, the mighty ship would never leave harbor.

"There are pieces of our world we would call inferior, an entire race of Trumen we Skullan would dismiss. We must be very careful, lest we discover we've thrown out not the empty crate, but the mainsail."

Walking through the Trumen workers, Tryst realized the truth of this. They were not mindless pigeons, rushing through life for their next handful of seed. In living amongst the Trumen, he found them much as Skullan, with dreams and goals. Fighting to live tomorrow while living today.

The Zaria scrolls were supposed to tell of three wars with the Trumen. Two had already happened; the third was something Minister Charis believed should be brought about. There was no doubt who would win, but much debate over the effects afterward. Many claimed it would purge the evil from the world; but there were those who thought it would purge the good as well. Destroy the sails, Jason had said.

Now as he strode toward the largest ship, dodging Trumen bearing sacks of flour and grain, he found himself with his own opinion. Tryst didn't know why the Trumen race existed, and he had no idea what truth the scrolls spoke. But he couldn't believe destroying a people for no reason was a good thing. Destroying Drail and his Hand of Victory, wiping out all the Old Merle's from existence. And the little Marra's. She was seemingly unimportant, yet Drail claimed it was she who woke him from a powerful sleep.

What possible good could come from destroying all that?

He stepped on the gangplank, and a beefy hand pressed his chest to stop him. "Your business with the Trafalcon?"

Tryst gazed up in annoyance at the Skullan sailor. He was used to Skullan treating him with respect, even awe. They kept proper distance, never near enough to touch him without his express permission. The smaller Trumen had touched him, of course, but somehow it had seemed part of a strange adventure.

Now he had no desire to allow such familiarity with his own race.

"That," he said as his grip locked the Skullan's fingers, "is between myself and the Captain."

Scowling, the sailor tried to yank free, and for his trouble found himself sinking to his knees, thanks to a leveraged fingerhold that Jason had taught him. Only when the Skullan quit fighting did Tryst release him.

"Do not step from the plank to the deck until given per-mission," the sailor warned him. Rubbing his hand, the man continued on down the wharf.

And Tryst walked up the plank. The ship was huge, the plank steep, so he couldn't see the deck until he reached the top. When he was with Jason, back all those years ago in Gold Harbor, he had merely walked onto the ship, and

men scurried to bow before him and offer refreshments. Today he heeded the sailor's warning.

Skullan swarmed the vessel, hoisting crates from the
center hold, swabbing down the exterior of the ship. The
Trafalcon, he reminded himself. Deck, rail, and rope cleat
all received the same wet mop and polish.

In the center of activity two men talked. Their clothes
were better than the sailors about them, and the work was
more enthusiastic nearby.

Tryst doubted they hadn't noticed him, but they continued talking. He in turn assumed a relaxed stance, taking his
time in surveying the ship. Ascertaining its worth. One of the
men broke out in a grin, and approached.

"How can we serve you, young master?"

"I seek passage to Missea."

The Captain's grin faded as he noticed Tryst's clothes.
Tryst had managed to upgrade his rags, but his appearance
was not that of an affluent man.

"And can you afford this passage? A hundred copper for
a birth?"

Tryst maintained his expression, even as his heart sank.
And realized there was no point. "Can one work for passage?"

The Captain nodded, eying his physique. "As long as you
carry the Mark." Quirking an eyebrow at Tryst's confusion,
the Captain continued. "No ship can take you without the
mark of health. A woman of Agben must mark you as safe
for the Grand Continent."

He meant Trumen, Tryst realized. Stars, Trumen were
treated like some sort of cattle, certified as healthy. It was

insulting. But even as his mouth opened to correct the Captain's mistake, the consequences of proclaiming himself Skullan flooded his mind. On this foreign continent, where few Skullan lived, without knowledge of who was friend and who was foe, did he dare reveal his identity?

And who would even believe him?

"It costs a gold coin to get such certification," the Captain added sympathetically.

Tryst nodded once, turned to leave. And then turned back. "I thank you."

The Captain strode away.

If the only way was to become Skullan, he would do well to shave and dress himself so before trying to board a ship. But it was doubtful he'd be believed even then. He was huge for a Trumen, but as a Skullan he was petite. Far, far better to remain a Trumen.

Tryst would speak to Old Merle, perhaps even nose around the taverns. But he suspected the mark of health was sacrosanct. And a gold coin – a thousand coppers – might as well have been the moon.

The Trial games were about to start, and Tryst was anxious to get to the Arena. Walking was difficult with twice as many pedestrians now as there were two days ago, when they first arrived. According to Old Merle, Port Leet would quadruple in population for the Solstice Game, the most important game on the Continent. These trial games were a first, and word had spread. Many were here early to watch.

Tryst himself had enjoyed going to the Gold Harbor Championship, the most prestigious game of them all. Only Skullan participated, and while he'd been brought up believing Trumen were a distant second to Skullan in all things, he could see a few advantages for them. Skullan tended to muscle everything, believing in the battering ram instead of the weighted push in the proper spot. But while Drail's strength among Trumen was undisputed, Tryst suspected his success lay more in his accuracy and sharp insight into his opponents.

He could almost believe they really had beaten the Skullan team on skill. Almost. But luck had played a part. At least Drail's team had escaped the necessity of playing in the Trials. In fact, they had a special box from which to watch.

Wagons and horses joined the march of pedestrians, making the streets difficult to cross. As he waited his chance, he spied Marra, and joined her. Startled, she did not welcome him.

"I wanted to thank you, little Marra," he said in all sincerity.

He'd accepted that he'd been drugged by some powerful Agben potion, but hadn't really considered his good fortune in waking. Naturally he'd assumed that he was supposed to wake up at that point, in the distant Flats, among enemies. Possibly for ransom.

Yesterday Drail had told him otherwise. The Trumen Captain swore he was as deep in sleep days into their desert journey as when they first found him. Marra, Drail insisted, had begun trying mixtures to counter the drug, and days later succeeded. Tryst still found that difficult to believe. But if true, it meant two very important things.

One, that Marra was not just a lucky apprentice. Indeed, Drail was the lucky one after all. To counter an Agben potion was no mean feat. In fact, he suspected Agben itself would be quite anxious to meet the girl.

And two, even more important, he was not supposed to be awake at all. Which begged the question exactly what was the plan? To kidnap him was one thing, but to so thoroughly hide the fact from his father suggested ransom was not the goal. Yet they had gone to a lot of trouble to keep him alive, to transport him so far away.

Marra's gaze brought him back to the present. He hadn't seen that lack of timidity before.

"Where are you from, Tryst?"

"Not this continent," he smiled ruefully. "Surely that is obvious."

"Which continent is your home?"

Startled, he studied her eyes, trying to ascertain her purpose. "The Great Continent – where else could it be?"

She never blinked. "There is the Dim Continent."

"I thought Trumen here believed that more myth than place."

Marra seemed to be looking through him, seeing what visions he could not guess. "If you are from the Great Continent, surely you would know. Is it myth? Or place?"

Yesterday he would have put her in her place. But today he was grateful, and not a little intrigued. He decided to honor her with truth.

"The Dim Continent exists, at least most in Missea believe it so. I have never seen it. I had a toy as a child, a stuffed creature with big eyes, called a Terrin. It was supposed to be from the Dim Continent, though I know no more about it. Come," finally a break in the road flow allowed the pedestrians to cross. "We don't want to miss the privilege of the Box."

His hand gently pushed in the small of her back, yet she did not move. For a second he thought she would refuse.

Then she obediently stepped into the street, and he shrugged off her odd behavior to ponder his own plight.

8.

DRAIL SURVEYED THE FIELD from the private box. And realized he was grinning like a desert fool.

The arena was surrounded by stair-step platforms, and these with benches for seats. He'd seen stands before, allowing multiple rows of spectators, but nothing like these. A full twenty rows surrounded the field, and each was well-able to see the game.

Better yet, above the rows were the boxes, a small room with padded seats and a back table with food upon it. Drail had heard tales of his grandsire and Port Leet, of the arena where a thousand faces could watch a single game. But he'd never known anything about raised viewing boxes.

And here he sat in one, a cool ale in his grasp, a clear view of the entire field. Which was a true comet field. For the first time he saw what his grandsire had described as a proper carved-out dip, the area scooped out so that the sides were a man's shoulder length higher than dead center, the comet tail. He had practiced on that field, and found his grandsire's words were true: in the heat of battle, the slopes rarely were felt, and the comet tail itself was made higher to compensate. But when a ball fell to the sand it rolled away, sometimes in unpredictable directions.

As Raston had said, it changed the game.

Manten, Olver, and Kayle climbed the steps, joining him at the rail. "Oh, sweet Desert Crane," Manten breathed, a look of wonder lighting his eyes.

Kayle gaped, faintly shaking his head. "So many," he whispered.

Manten clasped his shoulder. "That, my friend, is glorious."

Marra and Tryst arrived, and Drail briefly speculated on their relationship. Tryst was sneaking the odd look at her. But she seemed withdrawn, and as Tryst's presence held no effect that Drail could see, he dismissed the odd notion running through his head.

Even a mediocre game would seem grand in such a place. As the day wore on there were a few of those, but most games were average. Drail found himself relaxing. He'd harbored a suspicion that all these men would prove powerful opponents, and he'd feared the sheer number of them. His grandsire had said that winning a game was easy, but stringing wins together on an afternoon was difficult.

Chance played her part on the field, and given enough opportunity she would defeat you as surely as the men of a
superior team.

As the games continued, several mighty teams revealed
themselves. The four Skullan teams had all made the top
six, and now sat watching in their own boxes, as did the
other Trumen team. But two of the teams that had beaten
them in the past were on the field, and one was very good
indeed. Watching their skilled play, he felt no shame in having lost to them.

The Sandflats, that team who had killed a man and who
they had defeated, continued in a wild way. No one was
killed, but they showed an eagerness to maim as well as
win. One opponent stopped cold at the sheer viciousness of
their play, allowing their victory toss.

Bullies, Drail thought. Relying on fear in their opponents
to give them an edge. The Hand of Victory had beaten them
on their home field, and would not yield the day in Port Leet.

There was a team of wily veterans, with lines on their
faces and two with graying hair. But the muscles on their
bodies showed no sign of age, and their play revealed not
just power, but skill.

"That is a respectable opponent," Old Merle told them.
High accolades indeed.

"See how that young team there focuses only on the
ball," Merle pointed. "Their play becomes very predictable."

Drail watched carefully, knowing that his team's own victory could well depend on what they saw today. It was a
huge advantage to watch the others, to learn their moves

from the leisure of a box while they must fight to play on the Solstice. Even Kayle saw the advantage.

"I wonder if Spider-cheek regrets passing us through," Kayle stared across the arena, where the Skullan sported with drink and females.

"He passed you through," Tryst told him wryly, "because he doubted you'd make the finals otherwise. And he wishes to personally stomp you to death."

Seeing Kayle's face, Drail grinned. "Stomp in appearance, not in truth. And we've beaten him before."

Kayle did not look reassured.

Olver held out his empty cup – and for once, Marra did not move. Drail himself stood, grabbing the pitcher and doling out the remaining drops.

"We will need your elixir," he told her. A span of ten heartbeats thumped by before she nodded her head. She never looked at him.

And despite his excellent logic to the contrary, Drail found himself speculating again about her relationship with Tryst.

At the end of the day, ten teams won the right to play on the Solstice. The Sandflats were one, and Drail merely smiled at the chance to again put them in their place. Six others were good teams, but not such as Drail feared.

Three were outstanding teams, particularly the veterans. Old Merle had several ideas on how to play them, and Drail intended to heed his wisdom. When prodded, Tryst had also offered observations, and two in particular they would pursue. Tryst claimed to be no gamesman, but his insights were sharp and unique.

Tryst agreed to accompany them to work out. But little Marra slipped away before the dust settled from the final shot.

Marra hoped the shop would be empty. But it seemed the herb business in Port Leet was never still.

She weaved through the customers, finding her way to the boy behind the counter. "I must speak to her."

He gazed at her solemnly, and she almost told him who she meant, when he nodded and disappeared behind the curtain. The hand appeared shortly, beckoning. And Marra rounded the counter and slipped past the bright cloth.

Gran peered up at her sharply, but said nothing until Marra produced the crystal vial. "I need to know – that is, how would I tell if this substance –"

"It is," the old woman breathed. She cradled the vial, then held it up to the light from the broad window, one eye closed as she examined the white contents. "It is."

Unbidden, Marra slid down the wall to sit on a pillow at Gran's feet. She realized she had desperately hoped it was fake. "Are you certain?"

"Crystal vials," the old woman's voice was sharp, but her hand was gentle on Marra's shoulder. "Such vials are very expensive, even though their property is no different from simple glass. Crystal is designated by Agben for sanctioned contents only. To make their importance clear at a glance. This seal – it's pure beeswax, with the Agben symbol stamped atop. The symbol is Agben guarantee of the contents."

After all this time, to be handed Myrrcleft seemed far too generous of Fate. "It could not be forged? To fool the buyer?"

"I would give much to know what you paid for this," Gran eyed Marra sharply.

"It was a gift. Should we not open it? Examine the powder?"

The gnarled fingers held the crystal aloft again, slowly turning the glass. Marra watched, trying to see what Gran saw. The sun shone through the crystal, bouncing off the fine white powder within. Bits of it turned bright silver in the reflection.

"Once powdered, Myrrcleft will maintain its potency forever – it cannot go bad. As long as it remains kept in a glass vial. Nothing less. To open it would be to waste precious grains, for the smallest pinch is as rare as a fat waterfowl on the desert. You have enough here to last a lifetime.

"It's Myrrcleft. Of that much you may be sure, though all else from this giver might well be false."

The old woman held it out. Marra stared at the crystal and did not reach for it.

It was gently slid into her grasp.

Marra took a deep breath, and passed her the second vial. "And what of this?"

The old woman hefted it in her hand, weighing it. She held it up to the window light – and suddenly shoved it back at Marra.

"Will it kill?"

"That is a rare and powerful mixture, made for a purpose I cannot guess. Killing is a far too simple thing, easily done without such a crystal mixture. But I do not doubt this holds an evil intent."

Marra waited for more, but the old woman closed her eyes. "Leave now. Do not come back."

"If you want a share of the Myrrcleft –"

"No," was the abrupt reply. "I want no part of this thing you do."

Marra left.

She fled up the stairs to the Brista quarters as if Kratchett were chasing her. At the top of the landing she turned, half expecting to see him, but the hall was well lit with hanging oil lamps, and the light revealed she was alone.

Shaking herself as if to loosen from his grasp, she entered the quarters.

Bristas were accorded luxury that no gamesman would receive on the continent. A large welcome room, with soft chairs, reclining couches, and work tables all well-lit from the large windows and plentiful lanterns. Two of those windows were actually doors, opening to a balcony overlooking the city. The sheer extravagance of it all made her uncomfortable.

Off the receiving room were seven bedrooms, each with a locking door, a large soft bed and a window all its own. Marra had taken the first room she saw, only realizing later there were more. The rooms were spotlessly cleansed each day, with morning rolls and a pot of tea to break the fast, and a nervous serving girl to curtsey and offer her dinner each night.

It was a sanctuary of the finest order, worthy of a high lady. And overwhelming to a barefoot shop girl.

Now, standing on the threshold, she felt the change in atmosphere before spying the six leather bags lined neatly on the floor. Stars, who had so much she needed six bags to carry it?

A lady stepped out from the largest of the bedrooms. And smiled. "You must be the little herb girl they call the Desert Brista."

Marra could only stare. The lady was dressed full in velvet, from a soft cap on her glorious blond hair to the gloves on her hands that left her fingers bare. Jewels sparkled on her wrists and throat, as her eyes sparkled at some unknown jest.

And Marra suddenly wondered if *she* was the jest.

"I am Catrona," the lady said. "I was most interested in seeing you."

"You are Brista?" Marra asked. Fearful lest this powerful woman served one of the Skullan.

"I am of Agben," she answered coldly. And it was all Marra could do not to fall to her knees.

When she did not do so, Catrona stepped forward to tower over her. She was a tall woman, and Marra wondered briefly if she was Skullan. But other than the height, there was nothing Skullan about her.

"You will tell me now how the sleeping man woke in your care."

Marra's words stumbled over themselves to be first out of her mouth. "It was not the draught. I tried it for three nights, with varying leaf. I did not know what to do! It was unnatural, that sleep. When he woke – "

Whether from the lady's evil smile or her own running out of breath, Marra's pause lengthened, seeming all the louder in the silence that followed.

"Twasn't you at all, was it, little Desert Girl? Twas the natural variation for Skullan flesh."

Words trembled on Marra's tongue, of the inhalant she was sure had prodded Tryst to consciousness. But instinctively she kept her lips pressed together. And she trembled at her own temerity in not telling all to this woman.

Fortunately, Catrona was no longer watching her, but striding about the room in an almost masculine manner. "Kratchett is a fool. A scheming harlot betters her lot with a clover tonic, and he actually thinks a Brista is born on the Flats."

She whirled, finger leveled at Marra.

"You, bitch, have been commanded to put that princeling back to sleep. You will do so in three days. And then I might allow your pretense, while your little Trumen master wins a game or two."

With each word Catrona strode toward Marra, forcing her to stumble backwards, falling.

"Fail in your task, herb girl, and you will discover just what a true woman of Agben can do." Marra stared up, seeing the cold anger in the lady's eyes. Feeling her power as a tangible thing.

Marra scrambled to her feet and fled.

She had just dodged past the Tavern, going where she had no idea, when Marra literally bumped into Manten and Kayle coming the other way.

"Ho, Marra," Manten cried. "Let us buy you a warm stew, crusty bread, and a tankard of the finest ale in all the Flats."

"They feed me well in the Brista quarters." She tried to slip past, but Manten wrapped an arm about her shoulders.

"They don't feed us," Kayle told her.

"Because," Manten cuffed him playfully, "Gamesmen who are honored with a room in the arena are given food and drink everywhere. I suppose with Bristas it's different."

Marra nodded, even as Manten bore her back to the Tavern. "Come, let us honor you. All my life I dreamed of being a Gamesmen – and in just two days hence, we play in the Solstice. Drail swears we owe it to you."

She wanted nothing so much as to get away by herself. She needed to think. But they steered her back down the street. The double doors of the Gamesmen Tavern were larger than any she had seen, and propped wide open, the light and laughter inside spilling out to the street. As were the patrons – two men staggered backwards into her, apparently having meant to lean against a non-existent wall. They laughed, Manten and Kayle laughed, and Marra was swept past them into the crowded place.

In San Cris, the single Tavern held maybe thirty people if the celebration was very good, and rarely was it so. Men only went to the Tavern at the end of a work day, and then only if no greater use of the coin came to mind. In other towns on her journey she had found Taverns both larger and livelier, but here in Port Leet they teemed with men, and women. She doubted some ever made it home.

The size of the place stunned her. A giant square bar stood in the middle of the room, each side twice as long as the bar in her home town. Eight bartenders poured from various taps and still they barely kept up.

And the whole bar was polished wood. Wood was rare in the desert - more expensive than metal.

The noise was too loud, the laughter too harsh in her ears. She spun from the main bar, only to see Tryst himself, laughing with Drail over some foolishness. He actually stood up when he saw her, a hand flung out in welcome. Even as she shied away, Manten was propelling her towards him.

How could she possibly betray him?

Kratchett watched her enter the Gamesmen Tavern.

He sat in the shadowed area, at a small table against the wall. Here he could see all who entered and left, without being seen. It was his table now, after a week of patronage, and no one tried to argue the point.

The herb girl's expression was much the same as he'd last seen it – bemused, quiet. He would think her simple if he hadn't spoken to her. She obviously had the sense to keep silent about their little meeting, but then she didn't look ready to carry out her mission, either.

Catrona thought her simple. Catrona was no fool, but she did have a blind spot with women.

The little herb girl joined Tryst and the others, but remained quiet. A tankard was set before her, and her fingers played with the handle. But she didn't drink.

He nudged Lump. "Make her see you – lock eyes. Just for a moment." Lump drained his mug, then rose to stagger towards the bar, suddenly seeming much the worse for drink.

One of Lump's many qualities, he mused. The man understood, instantly and completely. Again Kratchett speculated on his past.

Lump walked with a drunk's carefulness toward the bar, then stumbled sideways, knocking into Drail's table. He bent over it – right in front of Marra – before one of Drail's men shoved him away. Little Marra paled, and Kratchett smiled. But he watched Tryst's face carefully.

Few in Port Leet would see anything but a drunk in Lump's movements, but Tryst was Prince of the realm. He had been taught to watch, to think. Still, Tryst seemingly did no more than laugh, and Kratchett decided he had not seen anything unusual. Tryst was playing a Trumen on a different continent, after all. And surrounded by big friends.

But Kratchett would to speak to Lump about taking greater care in the future.

Tryst saw the drunk staggering, and automatically arm-barred Marra back out of harm's way. He saw the swift, very sober look the man gave her, before Manten laughingly shoved him off the table. Tryst laughed himself, pretending to toast Manten as he studied the girl's face.

That was no accident. She recognized the man, and did not welcome the sight. And if the man could be that bold in front of them all, he must have some hold over her. He must want something from her, and that little performance was a threat.

The Hand of Victory, he thought. Someone wants them to lose, perhaps fearing the advantage a Brista gives them. She may have been threatened to see her elixir did no good this time, perhaps even hinder their game. Another team could be that anxious to win. Or even a merchant wagering on the outcome.

What could they have threatened to keep her silent?

Watching her unhappy face, Tryst vowed two things. One, he would do his level best tomorrow to prepare Drail and his team. He still thought beating Skullan near impossible, but perhaps these roving bands here were less disciplined than a Gold Harbor team. It would be interesting to watch the matches.

And two, if the Hand of Victory lost, it would be due to someone properly defeating them. Neither little Marra, nor anyone else, would hinder their game.

Perhaps it was good Marra ate her meal in the tavern. She might not have her vials, so even though they watched her, and threatened her, they must accept she could do nothing now. Surely they could not know she had her vials.

Her wonderfully safe quarters were no longer wonderful or safe. She doubted Catrona would have the slightest respect for personal belongings, and probably had in fact already examined Marra's things. What the woman would make of her small blanket satchel, when she traveled with so many fine leather bags, would be almost amusing. Almost.

Because when Tryst protected her from a simple drunk, as he thought, Marra had made her decision. She knew not where he came from, as she knew nothing of Fox Boots beyond what he claimed. But Tryst was a good man, with kind instincts.

And she would not betray him.

Mounting the stairs to the Brista apartments, she was very nervous. But she had no other place to go, and could scarcely explain it to Drail. The rooms were empty, however, and she hurried to her bed chamber.

Her blouse had been washed by the serving girl and hung on a peg. Her other things laid atop the bed, randomly scattered instead of the neat pile she'd left them. Marra patted the vials in her pockets, relieved now that she'd been reluctant to leave them behind. Obviously Catrona knew she had the sleeping potion, but she'd never mentioned the Myrrcleft, and Marra somehow doubted the woman would allow so valuable a thing to remain in her hands. Fox Boots must be very brave indeed.

Marra turned the key in her door, and realized she could lock it when she left in the morning. But locking it might make the woman wonder what she hid. It was probably better to leave it unlocked, and to carry her vials with her.

The serving girl had offered Marra an actual bath last night, and Marra had relished the hot water. She'd intended to have another one tonight, even though one hardly got dusty here. But she had no wish to be found naked in a tub when Catrona returned.

After splashing the cooling basin water on her face, Marra hung her skirt and blouse beside the newly laundered blouse, and climbed into bed.

Last night she'd happily promised herself new clothes. Tonight she swore to the Desert Crane that neither Tryst nor Drail would suffer due to her.

It took a long time to fall asleep.

9.

U P!" A VOICE ORDERED. It seemed to resonate in the tiny quarters.

Drail cracked one eye open. And saw Tryst, hands on hips, standing in the room center. "Is the arena on fire?" Olver muttered.

"Time to prepare," Tryst responded. "Losers lay about in bed, before and after the game."

Manten groaned. Old Merle, however, was sitting up, and Drail forced himself to rise and help the older man stand. "We should have the arena all to ourselves," Merle told him, shutting off any protests the others might have voiced.

The sun barely peeked over the horizon, but the arena was not empty. The Veterans, known as the Gray Warriors and a team Drail had already come to respect, were practicing full force. So were two of the four Skullan teams, and several others.

While we're abed our opponents prepare, Drail told himself. Good to remember that.

They began with stretches, loosening up. Old Merle walked around, watching the other teams carefully. A young team eyed him angrily and he moved on to the Veterans, who merely nodded and grinned.

"Why do they let Old Merle watch?" Kayle asked.

"Their strength lies in their skill, not gimmick moves." Drail observed the same grace and fluid motion he'd seen in the games yesterday.

"Note how they practice." Tryst said, watching with a light in his eyes. "They will give the Skullan a challenge they do not see coming."

"As will we," Olver insisted. Drail nodded once, and meant it. Win or lose, the Hand of Victory would give them all something to see.

After the warm ups, they ran around a portion of the arena, throwing the ball and shooting for the comet tail. The goal was usually accuracy, but today they were discovering the difference in a curved surface. It seemed to mean nothing in normal play, but the Tail itself was half a pace higher than they were used to, and Kayle couldn't quite see the hole.

"I can't play this field! This is ridiculous!"

Two of the Veterans grinned, and Kayle flushed red. Drail looked to Old Merle.

"It's just a simple matter of practice," he told him. "Your eye is used to judging from the hole – now judge from the cone itself."

"I'll never learn that by tomorrow."

"Then practice blocking, and feed the ball to someone else." Tryst told him, then leaned against the wall to watch the Skullan practice.

Olver scoffed, "A Gamesman must stand on his own. Everyone knows that."

Drail noticed, however, that Merle was giving Tryst that look again – a sort of startled respect, mingled with suspicion on just who this man really was. "The great teams come to know each other's strengths and weaknesses," Merle said slowly. "All men can shoot, of course, but some have better aim than others. Some are faster, bigger, or smarter at reading the opposition."

"Good men do it all," Tryst quoted. "Great men know their own strengths, and weaknesses."

Olver and Kayle both turned, annoyed. Drail cut them short by striding up to look Tryst in the eye.

"Show me," he said.

And there began a practice beyond any they had ever seen.

Marra woke to sunlight and panicked. But her room faced east, so it was early sunshine that danced upon her wall. The day was young.

She threw on her clean blouse, then listened cautiously. There were no sounds outside her door, and she could only hope Catrona was still abed.

Leaving her room, she again hesitated over the lock, but decided to leave it unsecured. The two crystal vials stayed in her skirt pocket.

The serving girl was just setting the tea on the table. She smiled at Marra. "Shall I wash your other blouse today, miss?"

Marra nodded, returning the smile. And then indicated Catrona's shut door. "Is she still in bed?"

The girl shook her head. "That one sleeps somewhere else."

Marra poured the tea, adding a dollop of honey. It was a rare treat for her, and she still felt guilty stirring it into her cup.

"Her team captain was looking for her earlier. He was angry to find her missing."

Marra grinned at the thought.

"She must be very brave, that one. I wouldn't upset a Skullan so, even if I was a Brista."

Marra stilled.

"And him with a Spider mark right on his face — I'd die before crossing him."

Setting her tea down, Marra stared at the girl. Then, "Can you fetch me some fresh spring water?"

The girl nodded, went for her blouse, then left the apartment. Marra bolted the door after her, and took down Britta's book from where she'd hidden it on the library shelf. Three rows of books were there, and she somehow knew it safer among them than anywhere in her room. By the time the girl returned with the spring water, Marra had measured out the Myrrcleft, and the book was back in its place.

She put the potion into a glass vial, and raced down to the arena.

The team was working hard, as were eight others. And Tryst was right in the middle of it, again. Drail winked at her as he ran past Manten to get the ball.

Marra held up the vial.

"We'll save that for tomorrow," he told her. She shook her head, and he finally called a halt to practice to join her.

"Marra, we don't need to take it today. It's just practice."

"This is a different formula. A better one, I believe. But I need to know that before you use it tomorrow."

By this time Tryst and the others had joined them. "The old formula works great," Drail leaned against the wall, emptying an entire skin of water.

"The Skullan have a Brista," she told him. And suddenly everyone was paying attention.

"Why do they need a Brista?" Kayle demanded, while Olver grimaced. "They must imitate us? I thought they only feared someone else would stomp us in half before they had the pleasure." Drail laughed, not taking any of it seriously.

"I can make the old formula, or I can make this," Marra urged him. "Try it now, and decide which it will be."

Drail looked at her, and nodded. Plucking the cork stopper from the vial, he hesitated. "Still drink one quarter?"

"Still drink one quarter."

He upended the potion, wiped his mouth, and passed it on. "It's - smokier," he said. Then he grabbed the ball and hurled it at Tryst. The two were back on the field, passing the comet faster and faster. With a shrug, Manten took his swig. The others drank in turn, though Kayle, last, sniffed it suspiciously before finally emptying the vial.

Kayle shrugged at her, indicating he felt no difference. And then he was off with the others.

Marra stayed to watch, partly to see if it did make a difference, and partly because she had nowhere else to go. She believed Catrona had dismissed her as unimportant, but Marra had no wish to cross her path again. No good could possibly come from that.

In the first hour Drail insisted there was no effect at all from the new potion. She was disappointed, and very surprised, but in a way that was comforting. Marra understood all the ingredients that made the old potion, but this new one, the true Birr Elixir, was well beyond her schooling. She had no way of knowing what subtle preparation techniques should have been used, or when – or indeed if – Britta would have judged her ready to learn.

In the second hour it all changed.

One of the Skullan had taken to knocking Kayle down at odd moments, pretending to not see him and laughing uproariously when he sprawled in the dirt. Kayle moved away from them, but somehow inevitably would be run over again. It happened three times as Marra watched.

It was just over an hour after the elixir, and Marra was contemplating seeking clothing with the two meager coppers she had, when the Skullan raced backward and plowed into Kayle. Kayle saw him at the last second, and stood his ground.

The Skullan literally bounced off him, lost his balance, and fell. Shaking his head, he looked up to see Kayle standing over him.

For an instant, Marra dreaded a huge fight, but the other Skullan burst out laughing all the more, one of them pounding Kayle on the back in that painful gesture she now recognized as male approval.

She began watching closely again, and thought Manten was moving faster. But she may have been imagining it.

And then Drail launched a shot from halfway out on the field – and it went straight in. Everyone in the arena went deathly still.

Drail threw back his head and shouted "KYYYYRRRRRAAAA!"

Slowly, very slowly, the other teams began to practice in earnest.

There was no guest box the following morning.

The Port Leet Arena had room on the edge of the field, and Marra and Tryst and Old Merle watched from there. All sixteen teams were present, though only four played. Boric, Keeper of the Games, called all team captains to the center of the field, to draw numbers determining the order of play.

"What is that?" Marra asked Tryst, trying to find the source of the sounds she heard. Tryst merely looked at her, having no clue what she was talking about, but Old Merle pointed to a center box. Four men stood with long gold horns, blowing into them.

"Trumpets," he told her.

She'd only heard music from strings, tied to a wooden device a man carried from town to town on the Flats. It had never occurred to her there were other musical instruments.

As luck would have it, Drail would play one of the Skullan teams in the second match.

As the first four teams battled it out – this group held two of the four Skullan teams – Marra gave Drail a vial of the old elixir.

Yesterday the true Birr Elixir had lasted three hours, which was not long enough to carry the Hand of Victory through all the games. So they had decided to use the old one first, and the new one before their second game. That should last through the final.

Assuming they made the final.

Marra felt foolish, for she had no real reason to deny use of the Birr Elixir twice in a day. But this Myrrcleft was something she didn't really understand, and it felt wrong to over-use it. Quite a debate had raged then, for some felt they'd need it to get into the final, while Drail insisted the final would be the time they'd need it most.

The trial games had been crowded, but today the sheer weight of the overflowing stands seemed to press into the earth. People sat comfortably in the boxes, while every-where else they squeezed in, standing on their feet, leaning hard into the rails that surely kept them from spilling down onto the field.

The trumpets sounded a single note. Spider-cheek and the other Skullan team roared out onto the field, seemingly larger than life. They faced two Trumen teams she'd never seen practice, and made very short work of them. Within ten minutes Spider-cheek scored first one, then the second comet. The third ball was sunk by the other Skullan team. And they both passed to the second round.

Leaving the field to wild applause, Spider-cheek mockingly shook a fist at Drail.

"The Skullan are very aggressive," Kayle muttered nervously.

"It might have helped if the Trumen had bothered to practice," Old Merle told him. "Flats teams. Used to sheer raw talent carrying them through, and never a thought that other teams might also have talent."

The second game was Drail's.

Old Merle solemnly tied the red cloth to the giant iron ring hanging behind them, as Drail marched to the arena center.

With the four captains at the tail, Marra again marveled at the sheer size of the Skullan beside Trumen. Then balls were hurled to the teams, and sand flew as everyone sprang into action. Perhaps these teams were better than the last, or perhaps they'd realized how aggressive the level of play could be. To Marra, it seemed as if they were all fighting for their lives.

This Skullan team had its members spread around the arena, playing close to the tail. Each continually blocked and harassed another team, foiling any attempt to score.

Kayle raced with the ball, aiming not for the tail but for Manten, when the Skullan flew at him full force.

Flesh smacked flesh; a sickening crunch was heard across the field, and Kayle collapsed into the sand.

Instinctively Marra started towards him. Tryst held her back.

"But he's hurt," she cried.

"They won't stop the game."

Laughing, the Skullan plucked Kayle's ball from the sand and hurled it at the tail. It missed.

But his teammate got it, ran up to the line, and sunk the ball. The normal crowd roar after each comet didn't follow — possibly the spectators were as uncertain as Marra felt.

Manten hovered around Kayle, eyes on his opponents, apparently talking to him. But Kayle never moved. Another Skullan roared up, without a ball, and Manten moved to block him. She realized he was there solely to keep his friend from being trampled.

The Skullan scored a second ball, and play stopped as they were escorted off the field. The applause seemed more for Manten carrying Kayle to the edge than for the Skullan victors.

Manten gently laid the unconscious man at Marra's feet, and whirled back to the field. "You can't play with three people.

"Watch me," he answered.

Kayle was unconscious, but breathing. Old Merle stepped in, his hands running over Kayle's limbs. For the first time Marra wished she was a healer.

"His arms and legs are whole." Merle ran hands along the torso, and shook his head. "Ribs are broken — at least two. We'll know more when the poor lad wakes."

She looked up as Drail hurled the ball to Manten, who launched himself towards the tail, determined to sink it. The other Trumen teams seemed slower, perhaps affected by the ruthlessness of the Skullan. Manten sunk the ball unopposed.

The last ball remained, and one of the young Trumen picked it up as an afterthought, trotting toward the center.

BAM. Drail plowed into him, grabbing the ball and streaking toward the tail. The other Trumen woke up, realizing his intent, and raced to stop him.

Blocked, Drail launched the ball a full ten paces from the tail. It went in.

And the crowd roared. Confused, Marra glanced at Old Merle. "But it doesn't count. Why are they cheering?"

"Hand of Victory sunk the last two balls. No matter what the scoring, Drail's in the finals." Tryst and Old Merle exchanged looks, then slapped each other on the back. "Only three men on the field. And Drail's in the second round."

"They cheer both Trumen and Skullan." Studying the stands, Marra guessed perhaps one spectator in ten was Skullan.

Old Merle grinned. "They cheer good play, strong men, and wild comets."

At the end of the fourth game, eight teams advanced and eight were out. All four Skullan teams had succeeded, as had the Sandflats and the Gray Warriors, and the Dockmen, a local favorite. And the Hand of Victory.

There was now a three hour rest before the final games.

The Arena had its own healer, a thin woman of uncertain age who ruled a windowless room with half a dozen beds. She said not a word, just waited for them to lay Kayle down, before running bony fingers the length and breadth of his frame.

Kayle was awake, and eyeing the healer with doubt. "Can't Marra do what needs doing?"

Ignoring him, the healer turned and disappeared behind a curtain. It was Marra who answered.

"I make potions – I know herbs. Someone has to determine what herbs you need to fix you."

The healer scuttled back with a tall pottery jar and wads of soft material. "What's wrong with him?" Marra asked. But the woman merely opened the jar and soaked a small cloth with the pungent liquid inside.

Drail touched the healer's arm. "What is wrong with him?"

She peered up into Drail's face, then touched her own throat. She was mute.

And seeing he understood, she turned to spread the small cloth over Kayle's ribs. "I knew it. Broken," Old Merle said.

Kayle grew wild-eyed as the healer pulled him upright, and wrapped more cloth tightly around his middle. "I guess I won't be playing this afternoon."

"No, my friend." Drail patted his shoulder, stopping when Kayle winced. "I think it's time for our teacher to give a practical demonstration of his methods."

Tryst had been expecting this, but not with enthusiasm. "There are now eight teams of experienced players with nothing to do this evening. Surely one of those would work much better in this instance."

Old Merle shook his head. "Most captains would not appreciate a teammate playing for another team, whatever the circumstances."

"Seems to me someone was just extolling the importance of learning your teammate's strengths, and playing to them. Only one man knows ours better than Kayle." Drail turned to face Tryst, meeting steady gaze to steady gaze.

"The prize money is very good," Old Merle grinned. "And each Winner receives the Mark."

Tryst snorted. Which they all took to mean 'yes'.

10.

MARRA WAS WORKING feverishly to prepare the Birr Elixir when Catrona unlocked the door and walked in.

Britta's book was back on its shelf, but the Myrrcleft sat right in the middle of the table. She'd finished adding all the ingredients, and was just in the process of gently shaking the vial. Catrona strode up to the Myrrcleft, lifted it, and glared.

"You still haven't performed your task."

Marra set the Birr down and approached the lady, hand out placatingly. "There has been no opportunity. With the games -"

Catrona slapped her hard.

Tears sprung to her eyes. Marra cradled the sore cheek.

"Don't lie to me, wench." The lady waggled the crystal vial in her face. "You fear to do the deed; you fear not to.

Your kind waits, hoping some third option will tiptoe up and tap you on the shoulder. Well, the only thing lurking at your back is trouble. Copious amounts."

Words trembled on Marra's tongue, but she held them back. Because in the rising tide of emotion, Marra wasn't sure what she might say. And all the while she watched the Myrrcleft in Catrona's hand.

"You could slip it in that silly drink now. It would all be over in an hour."

"All four will drink it," Marra told her. "One man unconscious will pass without comment – but the whole team?"

Clearly Catrona didn't want to concede her anything, but even she could see the point. She slapped the crystal vial on the table, and paced the rug.

"When the games are over, there will be much celebration. Tomorrow all of Port Leet will sleep late. Do the deed tonight."

Catrona marched to her room, returning with a shawl of delicate design. Marra's eyes fastened on the Myrrcleft vial back on the table. Catrona had thought it the sleeping potion. Marra couldn't even imagine what the woman would have done if she'd realized what it actually was.

"If you do not wear the signal scarf tomorrow morning – before noon, mind! – I'll have your back laid open with a lashing such as you've never dreamt of in your worst nightmare."

The woman strode to the door, then whirled back.

"And never lock this door again." The door slammed shut behind her.

Marra found her hands were trembling, and realized the words she wanted to shout were not excuses or cries for mercy. She'd wanted to tell Catrona off; she'd wanted to strike that cold face. She'd wanted to kick her shin, pull her hair.

Marra wanted, just once, to fight back. With a sigh, she realized that it wasn't a luxury she could afford.

Pocketing the Myrrcleft, she took the elixir and fled the room.

It was supper time, though Drail and his team had eaten earlier. Marra found them at the arena an hour before the game, as expected. They drank the Birr Elixir.

Tryst touched her chin to better see her cheek. "What -" he began, and she shook her head. He studied the reddening skin a second longer before releasing her. "We'll teach you a little of defending yourself," he told her, smiling. But he meant it, and it made betraying him all the more difficult.

The Summer Solstice was the longest day of the year. The sun would not set for hours yet, and the warmth of the day would not fade at all. The weather encouraged less clothing and more drink, compounding the festive atmosphere. And the games themselves spiced the feeling to a fevered pitch.

Tryst watched the stands fill. The excitement in the air, the laughing wagers, the cheering when a team appeared, or a man won a drinking game. They seemed to favor Skullan as well as Trumen, and he hoped that continued. Because he doubted a Trumen could possibly win the day.

Still, the Hand of Victory had gone far indeed. They may not win, but he vowed the loss wouldn't be laid at his door. When he saw Spider-cheek eying Drail, and whispering to his teammates, he felt that scathing regard he himself had felt for Trumen. The natural assumption that their lesser size made them lesser in all things. A dismissal of their race without truly seeing them.

Somehow he felt a burning resentment of it now, which was foolish. He was no Trumen. But if he'd been granted the chance to announce his identity, to climb the stands to a royal box and step into his birthright here and now, he wouldn't do it.

He wasn't sure, however, that he wanted to step onto the Gamesman field either. Conflicting emotions ran through him about pretending to be Trumen. Losing wasn't an issue – he expected that. And he welcomed the challenge. There was far too much in his current situation that he could do nothing about.

But if they managed to win this game, to go on to the final, it wouldn't be a genuine Trumen victory. Somehow that bothered him.

A massive cheer filled the air as Boric strode to the center of the field. The Judge raised his arms. "Team Captains! Approach and draw your lot!"

The eight teams would draw numbers to determine which game they played. Half would play first, half would play second. And the top two finishers of those games would play in the Solstice Championship.

Even in Missea, they knew of the Solstice Champion-ship.

Drail drew seven. It seemed the Hand of Victory would indeed have a chance to advance, for they would face only one of the four Skullan teams. The other three played in the first game, against the Sandflats.

And the leader of the Sandflats, that team that lived by intimidating their rivals, suddenly looked very intimidated.

The teams in the first game took the field, while the crowd's roar continued seemingly without end. The Sand-flats were already cowed, and Tryst felt disgust at their atti-tude. The Great Goose, leader of all constellations, usually served the very meal you requested. To assume defeat be-fore even taking the battlefield was the same as binding one arm uselessly to the side. You gave the enemy a great ad-vantage before even drawing sword.

It was a very hard fought game. The Trumen had already given up, and seemed to cower more than play, but the three Skullan teams were determined to win a place in the Final. The game lasted more than half an hour, but at last two victors stood. Spider-cheek was one of them.

And suddenly Drail was striding to the comet tail. In this game with only one Skullan team, a Trumen team must win through. For a moment Tryst almost wished they would lose. It would solve the concerns racing round in his brain. And then he saw the smirks exchanged between the Skullan.

He wanted the privilege of smearing those smirks across their collective heads.

Ball held high, Drail turned to face the field. Manten and Olver strode out to the center of their quadrant, perfect stances, shining eyes. This team, he realized, would not quit before the Judge called an end to the game.

They took pride in being there. And he found his pride in standing with them.

"COMET."

The ball hurled towards him, as did a Skullan. This was the team that liked to spread out and harass the others. But the man charging him seemed slow, and Tryst couldn't resist pretending fear, seeming to cringe, and then easily ducking past him to charge the tail.

Now the cone was undefended, but Tryst was not good at scoring. Seeing no teammates near, he threw the ball.

It bounced off the edge, came straight back at him. He heard the stampeding footsteps as he caught it, and dove sideways into a somersault.

The Skullan flew past, furious. Tryst wasn't sure if the fury was from missing him, or from another ball that went into the tail. Coming to his feet, he scanned the field to see Drail pumping a victory fist in the air. And turning to him.

Tryst hurled the ball his way – and it followed its brother into the cone.

"CEASE."

Pandemonium broke out as the Hand of Victory retired. Whether they won or lost now was up to the stars, but they had scored both first and second ball. He noted that the Dockmen team was nodding, and the Gray Warriors were actually smiling.

When the game resumed, the angry Skullan wasted no more time, but ran over two Trumen to score. And score again.

When the balls were plucked from the tail, it seemed the Skullan had won. They'd sunk the five ball, while Drail had but sunk the one. But thanks to the double scoring by the Skullan, no other team had placed.

The Hand of Victory would play three Skullan teams in the final game.

It was a scant quarter of an hour later, but it felt an eternity.

Drail took the field at the signal from the judge and the shouts from the stands. So many faces, so many throats screaming in anticipation. Excitement.

He belonged here. The Hand of Victory belonged on this field today.

He remembered a day with his grandsire, when he was so little that he could rest his head on the old man's knee. He'd just played comet with his sire and grandsire, and was happily weary.

"You belong on the field of champions," Raston had said. His father had responded, "Don't we all?", and left the room. To chase women or ale, no doubt.

But his grandsire remained, stroking his hair in a familiar, comforting manner. "Some men yearn to play. Some men deserve an occasional victory, a lucky shot before wives and friends. Some men want the chance to travel and play on far away fields.

"You, Drail, have more than that. You have that rare ability bestowed by the stars. The strength of the Cave Bear, the wiliness of the Desert Crane. The steadfastness of the Ancient Oak. And that loyalty earned among true friends."

Standing now inside the scoring ring, Drail selected a ball and turned to face his true friends. Manten, Olver, and yes, Tryst. He knew Kayle was not sorry to be on the sidelines. For whatever reason, the stars chose Tryst to stand in his place for this night. For this game.

"You're a champion, Drail." He heard his grandsire's voice as clear as he had on that long ago day. And he knew it for truth. He was no better than any other man. But each man had his strengths, and Drail's came from a line of champions. There was no purpose, Raston had said, in denying your strengths from modesty or foolish fears.

He thrust the ball high overhead, and the roar of the spectators was deafening.

He'd already won, he realized. He was playing in the championship.

"COMET."

He launched the ball toward Olver, who snatched it from the air and immediately raced toward the tail. No waiting, they had all decided. Score fast, score twice, and rest. That was Raston's creed.

Skullan seemed to prefer playing until the dirt faded from the ball, revealing which one held the high numbers. Tryst had said this had to do with a lack of faith in the stars – the Skullan did not like to leave anything to chance. It also made them vulnerable, for they unconsciously expected the same strategy from the Trumen.

Spider-cheek was sprinting towards him, ball in hand. Drail remembered how he loved to slam opponents with a comet shot. Drail leapt to avoid him – but Spider-cheek anticipated the leap, waiting until Drail was committed before spiking him. Drail curled and struck the ground.

The shot had been aimed for his head, and if connected would have rendered him as ineffective as Kayle. But although he hadn't been able to avoid it entirely, he'd managed to curl away, taking the strike on his shoulder.

Hitting the ground, he felt a surge of anger, of strength, and rolled upright before Spider-cheek had passed out of range. He took aim – and realized the foolishness of it.

He launched instead for the tail. A true shot, he felt in his gut, but it never had the chance to score. Another Skullan easily blocked it, whirled, and threw it to his teammates.

In his place Drail would have scored. They were indeed waiting to see which ball was which.

Then one of the Skullan hurled a ball at Tryst, who ducked. The ball bounced on the tip of the cone, rising gentle into the air, and then sinking into the tail. First score, and the Skullan looked unhappy.

Because it's done, Drail realized. Whether the ball was a five or a zero, that team was done. They could not change their score. If they had any sense, they would fight to sink another ball, just to reduce their opponent's chances.

A young Skullan on a different team sunk a ball quickly, as if fearing this situation. His leader cuffed him angrily for doing so.

And then Tryst came racing up from behind him. "Shoot!" he cried, tossing him a ball. Briefly Drail hesitated, wanting to wait, to see the numbers. But seeing the look on Tryst's face –

Drail sunk the ball.

And grinned. For in the last instant before it left his hands, he had seen two circles beneath the dirt. Placed such that the ball had to have three more circles. With the point for third place, they had scored six points. Against Skullan.

Manten sped off to snag the fourth ball, but was confounded when Spider-cheek himself sunk it. The game was over.

The cheering died quickly as the judge plucked the balls one-by-one from the cone, wiping each clean. Drail had indeed sunk the five, for a total of six points. But the one and zero point were the second and fourth place balls.

Leaving the three ball for first place. Spider-cheek had also scored a total of six points.

A tie meant a death game.

"Death game?" Marra asked fearfully.

Old Merle laughed. "You call it Tie Game. It's exactly the same – these two teams play until all four balls are sunk. Then everything is tallied, and the highest score wins."

Drail had never played a tie game as an adult, and had only just now realized the term death game meant a tie. He'd never associated those wild, fight-for-your-life stories Raston had told with the tie games boys played in the desert.

Even Raston called them brutal. Every score counts, unlike regular comet. Sinking the five ball first no longer guaranteed a win.

"Just keep scoring," Old Merle told him. "Each ball gives you a better chance to win – and you can't hurt yourself sinking a low ball."

Tryst and Manten nodded. Olver wiped the dripping sweat from his brow. "How long does that potion last?"

"Longer than you," Drail grinned.

Tryst up-ended a water bucket on an astonished Olver. "Cool off," he told him. "The end game is here."

"Victory is at Hand," Old Merle added. It was a joke, but Drail felt it in his bones.

Earnestly he faced his friends. Looking them in the eye, making them feel it. "Only one team stands between us and the Solstice Championship. One team only.

"And we have defeated them before."

11.

UNTIL THAT MOMENT, Tryst had never fully believed Skullan had lost to Trumen.

Now as they took the field, the crowd falling silent in anticipation, he knew they'd win. He knew it as a soldier knew victory at the dawn of battle. Not with the mind, but with the gut.

This time Drail held two balls – as did Spider-cheek. The balls were thrown, Drail letting both fly while Spider-cheek held one back.

And hurled it at Drail's head as soon as he stepped from the circle. Drail fell like a stone.

Manten and Tryst both raced towards him. And saw his eyes open again, saw him feel the offending ball beside him. He slowly rolled on his back, lifting the ball and tossing it gently.

It scored.

The stands erupted in pandemonium, and Spider-cheek froze. He'd been intent on retrieving the ball, never expecting Drail to be conscious. Never expecting that Trumen accuracy.

Manten slowed, grinning, but Tryst urged him on. "Score!" he hissed. And Manten started running again.

Frantic in his mistake, Spider-cheek gave up all strategy and sank the second ball, though it took him three tries. His teammates held off the Trumen. Tryst himself finally broke free, tossing the ball to Drail.

But Drail turned at the wrong moment, and the ball bounced high. Spider-cheek sunk a third ball as Tryst's came bouncing back to him.

Better to do something than nothing, Tryst thought, and threw the ball himself. It bounced off the tip, angling back towards him. Towards Drail.

Who now caught it and sent it flying again. This time it scored.

"CEASE."

The judge set Drail in the first spot, and Spider-cheek in the second. He then put another Skullan next to Spider-cheek. And pointed to him. To Tryst.

Hesitating only an instant, Tryst strode up to take his place in the fourth spot.

The judge plucked the last ball in from the tail, and strode to lay it at Tryst's feet. As the judge moved back to the cone, Tryst tried to see past the remaining dirt, to see the spots. He thought he saw one – but with the long shadows from the setting sun he really couldn't be sure.

It seemed to take forever for the judge to march back and forth, place ball after ball. The silence now seemed louder than all the earlier cheering.

At last the judge bent, rubbing the dirt from Drail's first place ball. "THREE," he announced. Cheers rose and quickly fell – the next two balls had been scored by Spider-cheek's team, and the five ball in either spot would negate Drail's first place spot.

Spider-cheek's first ball was cleaned. "ONE."

Even chance now, Tryst realized. If Tryst had sunk the zero ball, Spider-cheek won. He found himself watching Drail, his proud stance, his confidence. Was he so certain of victory? Or rightfully proud that win or lose, they'd held their own?

Then he stared as the judge cleaned Spider-cheek's other ball, watching, watching. Even as his eyes told him there were no spots, he didn't breathe until the judge announced it for all.

"ZERO."

The echoing roar was accompanied by a shower of ale. From the corner of his eye Tryst saw the other teams flood the field, the fans vaulting into the arena dirt to join them. But he didn't take his eyes off the judge until the final ball was wiped clean. Revealing the five spots.

If the judge announced the five, no one ever heard it.

His next thought was to clasp Drail's hand in the Trumen gesture of respect, but they were all born aloft on the shoulders of men he did not know, and carried off the field.

The celebrations had gone all through the night.

But in the morning, Marra was summoned to help Manten with his excess drinking, and gave him a rather useful potion. An hour later Tryst asked for the same treatment.

Now she walked the street, head down, nervously glancing out of the corner of her eyes. The scarf that man had given her was wound around her throat.

It took longer than she would have guessed, but he finally tapped her on the shoulder. "Where?"

"He's in the arena healing area."

"Go there. He'll be taken care of shortly."

Marra frowned. "But you don't need me."

"Be there." Lump told her. And she didn't dare disobey.

The healing room was empty of injured men. Marra had thought several would need attention, but only two besides Kayle had sought it, and those left as soon as they could.

Now only Tryst remained, lying so still. Marra stood by him almost protectively, watching Lump and a man she had never seen before enter. The stranger strode towards Tryst, but Lump bade him wait.

Fox-boots – Kratchett - entered last. And moved past the others to stare down at the unconscious man.

"I have you again, my prince," he smiled. Marra shuddered at his tone. "At least you had one last bit of glory. Lump, let's go."

Lump nodded at the other, who strode to Tryst's side. Marra backed away.

"Thoughtful of you to put him on the bed," Kratchett told Lump.

Lump shook his head.

"Well, the potion is instantaneous," Kratchett began slowly. "Little Marra could hardly -"

Drail and Manten came through the curtain; Old Merle, Olver and Kayle through the door. And as Kratchett plucked a dagger from his coat, Tryst himself grabbed his wrist.

Kratchett glared furiously at him, and then transferred that fury to Marra. "You have made a powerful enemy, harlot."

"So powerful he must threaten little girls?" Tryst swung his legs off the bed, shoving Kratchett aside as he stood. "Use frightened females instead of grown men to do his work?"

Marra was amazed to see Kratchett's dagger in Tryst's hand. She had no idea how he'd disarmed the man.

Kratchett clamped his mouth shut as Tryst looked him over carefully. "I know you," he said. "Kellan's man." When Kratchett said nothing, Tryst nodded. "Of course. Kellan betrayed me. But not, I think, without help."

"No one will ever believe you –" Kratchett closed his mouth again.

Tryst spread his arms wide, bowing. "I am but a humble Trumen."

"A Gamesman," Drail added. From his tone there was no higher accolade.

"The question," Tryst never took his eyes from Kratchett. "The question is, what are you?"

Suddenly Lump kicked Kayle's knee and punch Olver's solar plexus, dropping both men. He leapt past Marra, to snatch a broom leaning against the wall, and whirl it into a weapon.

The others reacted instantly. Kratchett yanked free of Tryst and sprinted out the door. Guarding his retreat, Lump then hurled it length-wise at Tryst, and fled.

The third man had stood gaping too long. He spun towards the door, but offered no resistance when Manten stopped him. "I know nothing!" he cried, his terror obvious. "They paid me to do a job is all! Carry a package – that was all!"

"Carry a package to where?"

"Down to the docks. That's all I know, I swear on the Desert Crane herself."

For the first time in his life, Drail wore his hair in a braid.

Having never done so before, he found plating his hair evenly a challenge. In the end he'd gone to Marra, who had done so without a word. The others had been more verbal. But they had won the Port Leet Solstice, and thus the right to wear a braid according to the Missean rules.

Drail swept them all to the harbor, still conscious of the dangling weight down his back.

On the wharf stood three imposing buildings, surveying the frantic activity. One was the Harbor Master, which controlled the docks. All ships reported to the Harbor Master to pay their fees and list their cargo.

The second building was the City Merchant Guild. No laws required a ship to talk to the guild, but somehow no profit was earned if one failed to do so.

The third building was tall and slender, with a high-sloped roof between two graceful spires. The roof was a brilliant blue, sparkling in the sun, and the spires were of a golden hue.

"A House of Agben," Tryst breathed. "I didn't know it was here."

They strode up the stone steps. Marra reluctantly waited as Drail pounded on the door.

And waited.

At last a tiny part of the door dropped down, and a fierce female gazed out at them. Old Merle stepped forward.

"The Hand of Victory, Solstice Champions, stand before you. We are here to claim the Mark."

The prize money was a great thing, of course, but it was the Mark that Drail wanted. He knew from Raston and Old Merle that today, the day after their victory, it would be easy to get Marks for Marra as well as the team. Today they would find ships bargaining for the privilege of carrying them to the Great Continent.

Tomorrow the opportunities might begin to fade.

The female now looked them over, seeming annoyed rather than impressed. But Old Merle wouldn't budge, and at last she opened the door itself.

They entered a cavern of a room, with a few couches, tables, chairs, and staircases on either side. There they waited for an hour, until the female returned with an old woman.

It was Gran from the herb shop.

Drail knew they could stay in the finest room in the finest inn for free. All of Port Leet was open to them. But he intended to leave on the first good ship that sailed. For now he had the Mark of Health tattoo, and the Port Leet Solstice Champion symbol stitched on his leather. He would play the games on the Great Continent, like his grandsire before him. Old Merle warned it was a whole new level of play. He didn't care.

It was his dream, and that was enough.

Tryst had seemed nervous of getting his Mark. Drail wasn't sure if it was a hesitation to join the Hand of Victory, or a wish not to be beholden. Kayle, however, did not want to leave the Flats, and they could hardly choose a better man than Tryst to replace him.

When the old woman looked Tryst over, she frowned and clucked numerous times. Finally she stepped back from him, hands on her hips. "You wish a Mark?"

"We need it to travel," Drail told her again.

Tryst looked into her eyes. "All Trumen need marks to go to the Great Continent. And I must go there."

She cackled, and stepped away. A moment later she returned with large copper disks. "This one cannot be tattooed," she announced, and handed Tryst a disk. "So if you insist on your folly, do not lose this."

"Marra goes as well," Drail told her, but she tattooed the girl without so much as prodding her to open her mouth. "This one," she said as she pressed the disk in Marra's palm. "This one must travel." And when Marra smiled warmly at her, the old woman patted her cheek.

Marra held back as the others filed out. Gran cocked an eyebrow, waiting.

"You're a woman of Agben, then?" Marra asked. Gran smiled softly, and for a moment her gaze was far off.

"I was called in, to do this task."

They left the room, descending the stairs together. And as they walked Marra studied the Agben House, noting the width of the steps, the large hallways, the numerous seats luxuriously padded. And all empty.

"Where are the Agben women?" she asked quietly.

Gran continued across the marble floor to the double doors. Marra quickly followed, not wanting to be left behind. Only when the door was closed, and they stood in sunshine, did Gran speak.

"Apparently they left, two weeks ago. Recalled to Missea."

Drail and the others were already halfway to the wharf. "Does that happen often?" Marra asked.

The old woman shook her head. "Never. No Agben House has ever been deserted like this."

Gran glanced over her shoulder, then leaned in close to Marra. "I don't know what it means, girl," she told her softly. "But every possibility I can think of scares the sand right out of my bones."

Epilogue

THAT AFTERNOON the Hand of Victory, with its trainer Old Merle and its Brista Marra, visited the docks. They found a fine schooner called the Trafalcon, with a strong Captain, a large cabin for the team and a small private room for the woman. When the Trafalcon sailed in three days, they would sail with her.

Old Merle produced a suite of rooms at the Victory Inn, including a beautiful chamber for Marra. She had but to gather her things from the Brista quarters.

Nervously she entered the apartments, relaxing as she saw they were empty. Her second blouse hung on its peg, laundered by the serving girl. Instead of taking it, Marra hung her old skirt and first blouse beside it. Drail had insisted on giving her coins from the prize money, and she had finally bought new things to wear, of linen cloth and actually dyed to pretty colors. Not velvet, perhaps, but fresh and bright and new. She realized she'd never worn new things in her whole existence. Her mother had always stitched old clothes into a proper size for her daughter.

She debated leaving her shoes – they were just sandflat sandals, after all, and the serving girl might not appreciate them. But in the end she did leave them. If the girl didn't want them, she could do with them as she wished.

With her new bag Marra packed her herb sashes, her vials, and the Myrrcleft. The bag was cloth, not leather, but it had a drawstring that looped over her shoulder. She moved to the library shelves and was just pulling Britta's book free when the door opened.

Catrona stood there, hands on hips, eyes burning with anger. Marra instinctively pushed the book back, and could only hope the woman hadn't noticed it.

"You bitch." Catrona slammed the door, strode up and slapped her. "You little bitch. Do you have any idea the trouble you caused?"

Trembling, cradling her cheek, Marra watched the lady turn to the bookshelves. "Now what do we have –"

Clenching her fingers as Tryst had shown her, thumb on the outside so not to get injured on impact, Marra swung her fist into Catrona's jaw.

The woman dropped with a thump.

Beyond her, the door stood open and the serving girl entered. She took in the unconscious lady on the floor, then stared at Marra.

And smiled.

Startled and feeling guilty over her action, Marra found that smile reassuring. Returning the smile, she plucked Britta's book free of the shelf.

"I've left a few things in the room for you, if you want them."

"You're very sweet, Miss." the girl stepped over Catrona's inert form. "Very sweet."

She disappeared as Marra stuffed the book in her bag.

Tryst had offered to teach her how to defend herself, and she'd hesitated. Somehow it seemed once you crossed that line there was no going back. Marra had feared the thought that even more punishment would come her way. That somehow she'd be asking for it.

But she had never asked for it, she realized. Perhaps it was time to quit allowing it.

Stepping over the lady of Agben, Marra left the room and the arena. Very soon she would leave the Wavering Continent, and all she'd ever known.

End of Book 1

THE AGBEN SCHOOL

Book 2 of The Legend of the Gamesmen

It should have been a happy ending.

A Prince restored, victory in the black arena. Instead the band of friends shatters against an evil conspiracy.

Refusing to endanger one man or burden another, Marra flees to the Agben School. Agben, whose ancient walls have held for a thousand years, protecting those within as they sought to harness the power of nature.

But this evil is relentless, and the school may not be the safe ground she thought. In fact it may not be anything she thought. Cut off from the only friends she knew, Marra discovers more than her life hangs in the balance.

For the future of her race – of both races – depends not on a prince trying to save his people, nor the heroic men who'd brought them this far.

Everything depends on *her*.

THE DIM CONTINENT

Book 3 of The Legend of the Gamesmen
Series Finale

Agben taught the art of using herbs to heal or enhance. Yet Marra saw one woman's brews detect a passing prince and cloak a creature's true appearance. A forbidden discipline - and being wielded against Tryst's throne.

The key ingredient grows only on the Dim Continent.

Journeying with her mentor to this fabled place, she stumbles on another secret: that the Women of Agben include Terrin - the same hairy creatures that kidnapped a king. Now the trust that bound the two species together is rapidly corroding.

Marra doesn't know Prince Tryst has also pursued the traitors to this wild, dangerous land. Or that Drail travels with him, to provide gamesmen cover.

In a land of strange beings and dangerous animals, Marra, Tryst, and Drail must again pool their skills, this time not just to save themselves – but to save all their people. The fate of Skullan and Trumen alike depends on defeating a powerful enemy who has plotted their destruction for centuries.

The final battle looms in the evil heart of power – the Dim Continent.

ABOUT THE AUTHOR

Jo Sparkes, a well-known Century City Producer once said, *"...writes some of the best dialogue I've read."*

Jo graduated from Washington College, a small liberal arts college famous for its creative writing program, and went on to study with Robert Powell: a student of renowned teachers Lew Hunter and Richard Walter, head of UCLA's Screenwriting Program.

She's won a Kay Snow for her comedy script, 'Frank Retrieval', a Silver IPPY for 'The Birr Elixir', and BRAG Medallions for multiple books. A member of the Pro Football Writers Association, she was (unofficially) the first to interview Emmitt Smith when he came to the Arizona Cardinals.

Jo served as an adjunct teacher at the Film School at Scottsdale Community College, and even made a video of her most beloved lecture. Her book for writers and artists, "Feedback How to Give It How to Get It" has garnered strong praise.

When not diligently perfecting her craft, Jo can be found exploring her new home of Portland, Oregon, with her husband Ian, and their dog Oscar.